ENDURING MAGIC

THE THORNE WITCHES HEA BOOK 1

T.M. CROMER

ISBN: 978-1-956941-20-3 (ebook)
ISBN: 978-1-956941-21-0 (paperback)

Cover Design: Deranged Doctor Designs

Editor: Trusted Accomplice

"We have a problem, C.C."

Cooper Carlyle hung his head and heaved a put-upon sigh. The last time this happened, he ended up in a relationship with a beautiful, zany witch. She'd turned out to be the love of his life, but the drama associated with her family was never ending.

After a moment, he turned off the burner, put down his spatula, and faced his brother. "What is it, Keaton?"

"The squirrel mafia."

"What's Saul done this time?"

Keaton moved in on Coop's bacon and snagged a slice. "He's making eyes at Chloe's new rabbit."

"Fucking Saul!"

"Ucking Saul!" a sweet little voice repeated.

"C.C., try to remember my son is a parrot," Keaton warned.

"I'm a parrot!" Jolyon shouted from his high chair, with one fist in the air and the other wrapped around a mashed-up pancake.

Coop gritted his teeth in a semblance of a smile for the kids' sakes. "Fucking Saul," he muttered in a low voice so his nephew and his daughter, Olivia, wouldn't hear.

"I think that's what he wants to do with the rabbit," Keaton returned dryly.

Coop rolled his eyes and snorted. "I promised Summer I could handle her beasts while she was off with her family."

"Yeah, well, how do you think I feel? What am I supposed to tell my daughter when she comes home to mutant baby squirbits."

"What the hell is a squirbit?"

"An animal that is half squirrel, half rabbit."

"Squir-bit!" Jolly shouted as he banged his palm on the chair's tray. "Squir-bit! Squir-bit!"

Olivia, little angel-faced cherub that she was, laughed at her cousin's antics. Jolly and Ollie were partners in crime and practically inseparable.

Coop couldn't keep his own laughter contained. "I don't claim to be a vet like Summer; however, I doubt you need to worry about baby squirbits." He picked up his coffee and sipped it. "But I promise to ask her when she calls tonight."

"Good, because if it's a thing, I need to know. In the meantime, talk to him, man, okay?"

"Sure, but I can't promise he'll listen to me. Saul is Summer's familiar, but he's got a screw loose. I don't even pretend to know what goes on in his pea brain."

Keaton's eyes widened as he locked onto something just beyond Coop's shoulder.

A sinking sensation started in his chest and ended somewhere around his butthole. "He's behind me, isn't he?"

Saul's tough-guy accent was pure Goodfellas when he said, "Sleep with one eye open, mudder—"

"Children!" Coop shouted to drown out the f-bomb at the end of the squirrel's tirade. Never mind that he'd just forgotten himself and swore a minute ago. The feral snarl on Saul's face told Coop he'd be lucky not to be whacked by the furry thug in his bed tonight. "Now, Saul, Summer wouldn't like to come home and find me dead."

"Dead? Who said anything about killing you?" Saul puffed out his little chest. "I'm just going to do to you what I should've done the first time you hurt my girl—cut your balls off!"

Coop cupped himself. "No! There will be no cutting off balls in this house."

The atmosphere around them thickened, and the crackle that followed was an indication of an incoming witch or warlock. But Coop didn't take his eyes from the rabid squirrel. As a veteran sheriff with a number of years under his utility belt, he knew when a threat was real.

"Stand down, Saul." Alastair Thorne had a commanding quality that brooked no argument. When he spoke, people—or in this case, animal familiars—listened.

Saul darted a resentful look toward Coop, gave Alastair a short nod, then scurried away. Or almost away. He stopped a few feet behind Summer's father, met Coop's eyes, and ran his paw across his throat in a cutting action.

Sweat broke out on Coop's lower back. He was definitely sleeping with one eye open from here on out.

"He's a squirrel, boy. He can't really hurt you." Alastair's amusement got under his skin.

"He's a familiar that carries a rusty razor blade and a grudge."

Alastair laughed and clapped him on the back. "When I talk to my daughter, I'll be sure to tell her you let the little rodent run all over you."

"Of course you will." Coop picked up his spatula. "What brings you by today?"

"My granddaughter." Alastair bent over and chucked her under the chin. "How is my darling poopie-doop Olivia?"

Had Coop not heard it, he would never have believed Alastair would ever stoop to anything remotely like baby talk. He opened his mouth to comment, but he met his brother's alarmed gaze across the expanse of Alastair's back. Eyes wide with something akin to terror, Keaton frantically shook his head.

Coop clamped his mouth shut.

"Wise decision, son," Alastair said as he waved a hand to magically change Olivia into a clean onesie before lifting her from her high chair. When she was settled in his arms and happily tugging on his nose, he grinned. "Don't think I didn't feel your snarky comment forming, Cooper. Your animosity builds and becomes a pain in my left butt cheek."

Coop desperately wanted to retort, but turned back to salvage the food on the stove instead.

"Why in the name of the Goddess are you cooking when you can conjure?" Alastair sounded as if Coop had decided to grill cow patties.

"I happen to like cooking, and what is it teaching my child if she doesn't learn to function like a normal adult?" He glanced over his shoulder in time to witness the distaste on the other man's face.

The pained expression on Alastair's visage spoke volumes. "Olivia, my little muffin. What do we tell your father when he insists on treating you like an ungifted mortal child?"

"Witch! Witch!" she cried happily, patting her palms against each of her grandfather's cheeks.

"Precisely." Alastair grinned at her, and the love shining from his sapphire eyes made Coop remember why he didn't argue against his future father-in-law popping in whenever he felt like it. Olivia had a mutual adoration for Alastair. "You are the smartest little witch on the planet, my dear girl."

"Witch is the only thing she says other than Mama," Coop said with disgust. "You'd think Daddy might be easier than witch, but no. Not for my kid."

"She shouldn't be talking at all at this age. She obviously gets her smarts from her mother's side."

Coop ignored Alastair's droll comment as he chowed down on a slice of bacon. "Where's Rorie?"

Usually, the man never went anywhere without his mate. After an almost twenty-year separation, the two were practically attached at the hip. Only in severely dangerous situations would Alastair leave her behind so he could neutralize any threat.

"She decided to go with her daughters on the cruise."

Coop had picked up his coffee cup but paused with it halfway to his lips. "I'm surprised you let her."

Alastair's sharp bark of laughter echoed around the kitchen. "Son, have you met my wife? I don't let her do anything. She'd make Summer's rabid rodent look tame should I dare try to tell her what to do. And I like my ba—" He glanced down at Olivia. "Er, man bits, exactly where they are. Besides, I went on the cruise with her. I teleported at Summer's urging."

"She doesn't think I can handle things without

her?" Indignation curled Coop's free hand into a fist, and he tightened his grip on his mug.

"No. She has great faith in your abilities. I, however, do not." Alastair blew a raspberry on Olivia's smooth, pink cheek. "I'm afraid I scared her into thinking you might burn the house down around you."

"I almost caught the barn on fire once when I was first learning. Once. And it all worked out okay." Coop was still defensive about the incident because Alastair liked to taunt him whenever possible.

"You really are a joy to rile, my boy." With deep affection, he ran a hand over Olivia's blonde curls. "Be good for your father, poopie-doop. He's still as much a novice as you."

"Gee, thanks," Coop muttered darkly. He held out his hands for his daughter and felt a smidgeon of satisfaction when she dove into his waiting arms. He kissed her upturned face and cradled her against his chest. "Olivia doesn't judge her daddy. Do you, my heart?"

"Witch!" she replied.

Coop chuckled. "Okay, maybe you do a little, huh?"

"Witch!"

He gave her a gentle squeeze because it was impossible not to. "Witch is right. Are you ready for your nap, my little witch?"

"At this hour?" Alastair frowned and glanced at his watch. "It's only half past ten."

Although he was loath to admit it, Coop said, "She

was up most of the night. I think she misses Summer."

"Understandable." The gentleness in Alastair's voice caused Coop to glance up. "I've been through it with my three. Sometimes, only a mother's soothing presence will do."

"Yeah. It took me forever to get her down to sleep last night."

Looking at Coop as if he'd lost his damned mind, Alastair shook his head. "Son, you are a magical being. At any time, you could utilize a spell to put her to bed and save yourself the grief. Why you insist on going down a magicless path is beyond me."

Keaton chuckled. "It's beyond all of us." He peeled the last of the pancake from between Jolly's fingers and waved a hand to clean his son. With a taunting grin for Coop, he said, "So much easier."

Alastair gestured with his thumb. "See? Even the slowest member of your family agrees." His lips twitched as if he fought a smile when Keaton began to sputter his objection to being called slow. "And on that note, I'll leave you all to it. I have an umbrella cocktail waiting back on the ship."

"Umbrella cocktail?" Coop and Keaton asked in stereo. They shared an incredulous look.

Coop turned back to stare at Alastair. "Since when do you like umbrella drinks?"

"Oh, I don't. I simply said I had one waiting back on the ship. I need to return and make it seem as if I'm enjoying it to appease Rorie and the girls. It's really a simple glamour to hide my scotch." He chuckled, and the sound lingered moments after he teleported away.

"Well, that was fun," Coop said, lifting Olivia to take a tentative sniff of her bottom. He shifted her until they were eye to eye. "Now I know why your papaw left so suddenly."

"Papaw?" Keaton laughed uproariously. "Does Alastair know you call him that?"

Coop gave his brother an evil grin. "Not yet. But he will when Olivia is talking full sentences."

"Dude. You have a death wish."

SUMMER RAN a hand over the mirror to wipe away the evidence of her scrying. Turning to her mother, she smiled. "At least they didn't kill each other."

"Papaw!" Aurora crowed. Her tinkling laugh warmed Summer's insides. Never would she get tired of hearing her mother's beloved voice in any capacity. Too many years had been stolen from them due to a stray bullet meant for her father's heart. The fact her mother was standing before her now was a miracle of epic proportions.

"Do you think Dad really believes we don't know he's switched out the rum runner for his Glenfiddich?"

Her mother gave an elegant shrug. "One never knows with your father, dear. But let's go back topside because he'll be searching for us."

"You go ahead. I'll be up shortly."

"You can nap just as easily in a lounger." Aurora smoothed back Summer's hair. "The exhaustion on your face tells me you didn't sleep all that well last night, either. The first time you're away from your child is worrisome, isn't it?"

"It is. I didn't think it would be so hard, Mama." Summer sat heavily on the edge of the bed. "I haven't spent a night without Coop in almost two years. And now with Olivia…" With a grimace, she asked, "Am I being pathetic?"

Her mother's soft smile assured her she wasn't. "Take your nap. I have other ways to entertain your father." Aurora winked just before she sailed out the door.

Envisioning Coop's old bedroom at the Carlyle estate, Summer closed her eyes and allowed her magic to warm her cells. When she lifted her lids, she was standing in the center of the room. It took only a moment to find Coop in the nursery, rocking Olivia as she played with his chin.

He glanced up as Summer entered, and his wide, pleased smile filled her with untold joy. It would always be so, this happiness to see him.

"Hey, sweetheart." His gruff, sexy-as-hell tone curled her toes.

"Hey." She touched a hand to Olivia's silky blonde locks, then dropped a soft, lingering kiss on Coop's welcoming mouth.

"Shouldn't you be sitting by a pool somewhere as your ship speeds toward the islands?" he teased.

"Yes, but I didn't realize how much I'd miss you both."

"It's only been eighteen hours." He rose and set Olivia in her crib before turning to take Summer into his arms.

"Tell me you slept like a baby while I was gone, and I'll teleport back."

"I didn't say that. Both Olivia and I had a rough night of it." He yawned and scratched the stubble on his square jaw. "As a matter of fact, I was going to try to sneak a few hours' sleep, myself." His steel-blue eyes heated to molten metal as they dropped to her lips. "Care to join me?"

Summer giggled and wrapped her arms around his neck. "I thought you'd never ask."

Placing a finger to his lips, he clasped her hand and tiptoed from the nursery. When they got to the hall, he raced with her to the bedroom he was currently using. Ducking inside, he shut and locked the door. "Get naked, woman. Based on past experience with your daughter's timing, we have to make this quick."

All her fatigue disappeared in the face of his desire. Lifting her hand, she snapped her fingers, divesting them both of their clothing. "Quick enough for you?"

"Boy, was it ever!" He scooped her up and dove for the bed amidst her gales of laughter.

---

2

*C*oop trailed his fingers up and down Summer's back as she sprawled across his pleasantly sculpted chest. Both of them were breathing hard, recovering from "nap time."

"Should I text your brother to ask if he'll listen for Olivia while we *really* sleep this time?" she asked, placing a featherlight kiss on his muscled pec.

"I've got it." He reached for his cell and tapped out a message as Summer closed her eyes.

"You know, we have to decide what we're doing for your little angel's first birthday this year." She yawned and rolled onto her back, bringing the sheet up to her chest. "We also have to stop my father from buying her everything like he did for Frankie's first birthday. My sister practically had to build a spare room for all the toys."

Coop chuckled and rolled on his side. Tucking his

hand under his head, he stared down at her. With the edge of the sheet, he traced a random pattern over her breasts, pausing to lean in and kiss her hardened nipple. "I'm not opposed to Ollie being spoiled, in the least. It's the one thing your father and I agree on, but please, never tell him that."

"Promise." Summer reached up and ran her nails across his scruff. To her, he was sexier when he was a little unkempt. The messy hair and a couple days' growth of beard told her he was in easy-going-Coop mode, the not-so-uptight-sheriff version of the man she loved.

"When do you head back to the ship?" he asked absently.

"I'm not in a hurry. Mama knew I was planning to take a nap, and I suspect she also knew that nap would be here."

Coop's lips twisted in a semblance of a smile, and he flopped down. "Back to the birthday discussion. Keaton and Autumn want to host it here. Do you have a problem with that?"

"Not really, but Dad might. I'm sure he'd prefer somewhere a little more fortified, like Thorne Manor or his place in North Carolina."

"We could host it at our home"—he paused dramatically—"along with a wedding."

Thoroughly shocked, Summer's eyes flew wide. *"What?"*

Of course they'd discussed marriage, their engagement was proof, but it had never been quite the right time, with one challenge or another popping up for her family.

Coop rolled to his knees, a small black jewelry box in his hands. "This is merely a formality since you've already agreed once before, but will you marry me, Summer Thorne?"

Giddy, she knelt in front of him. "You know I will."

Nestled inside the box was an antique-looking silver locket decorated with gold filigree on the front. With great care, she removed it and eased open the lid to display a picture of their little family. Coop had Morty in one arm and embraced Summer, who held Olivia, in the other. Behind them, perched on Eddie's trunk, were Saul and Rocco.

"It's beautiful, Coop! Thank you."

"It's not the engagement ring you were expecting, I know, and I still intend to conjure one for you when I develop the skill. But that was my grandmother's locket, and I wanted you to have it." His shining eyes lost a little of their sparkle, and he pushed his hand through his thick blond hair as he sighed. "I still miss her after all this time. You never got to meet her, but she'd have loved you, Summer."

She bit her lip and looked up at him from under her lashes, weighing how he would take her next comment. There were quite a few things his parents had wiped from the memories of the Carlyle boys in their effort to suppress their magic and have them live what they considered normal, non-magical lives.

Knowledge of their witchy neighbors, the Thornes, was one of them.

Summer's parents had cloaked their estate when she and her sisters were young. Only after they felt she and her sisters were old enough to control their abilities did they remove the glamour from Thorne Manor and let it be known they were all in residence. It was during high school that Summer met Coop for the third and final time.

But her love for him had been established long before. Back when a kind little boy gave a tearful girl, who had just dropped her ice cream in the dirt, his own cone to make her smile again.

After a time, Coop had forgiven his parents for suppressing his abilities, but he still grew salty at learning things after the fact, and Summer hated to spring this on him.

"Confession?"

He frowned but nodded.

"I met your grandmother."

"*What?* When?"

"She would come to visit my mother when we were small children, and she'd bring a lemon pound cake with this amazingly tart lemon frosting." Summer smiled at the memory. "We were like a pack of ravenous wolves and devoured every last crumb whenever she'd pop over. Mama adored her."

"I never knew."

"I'm surprised because your gran brought you with her once."

He appeared dumbfounded. "I don't recall."

"I think I was about six, so you'd have been slightly older. You were in time-out, pouting on the steps because you didn't want to play with 'dumb ol' girls.'"

His frown cleared, and wonder lit his eyes. "I actually remember that! Grams refused to allow me any cake because I'd been a 'right brat,' according to her. One of you—wait! Not *one* of you. It was *you* who snuck around the side of the house and gave me yours."

"I felt bad you didn't have any," she said with a laugh.

"And I feel bad I never recognized how sweet and generous you were even then," he said softly. "How did you ever forgive me for being such an ass to you all those years, sweetheart?"

She looked down at the locket in her hand and turned it so the picture faced him. "It was all worth it, don't you think?"

"Yeah. It definitely was." His voice was gruff, and there was a sheen of tears in his eyes.

"Coop?"

He cleared his throat and lifted a brow in question.

Summer shook her head and gave him a tender smile. "You really need to stop blaming yourself, you know. The Eddie incident, the arguments, and the split... accidentally shooting me. It all got us to this moment." She cupped his jaw and pressed her forehead to his. "And to that beautiful baby in the other room."

"I know, but whenever I think of how close I came to losing you through my own stupidity..." He shuddered and closed his eyes. "Christ, Summer. It's a wonder you didn't pull a Spring and bury me."

"Let's not talk about the past anymore. I don't want it to ruin your second proposal." She handed him the locket and turned her back to him. "Will you put it on me?"

He complied with a kiss on her shoulder. "Let me see."

She faced him and tipped her head to look as he straightened the chain and settled it between her breasts.

"Perfect," they said in unison. Their gazes locked, and they both grinned.

"I love you, Cooper Carlyle."

"And I love you, Summer Thorne-soon-to-be-Carlyle." He leaned in and placed a firm kiss against her mouth. "And I've changed my mind. I think we should get married at Thorne Manor as soon as possible. On the front lawn, by the steps where you gave me the lemon cake. If that works for you."

Overcome with love, the raw emotion clogged her throat, making speech impossible, so she simply nodded her agreement.

"I'll inform our families while you're on your cruise. When you get back, we'll plan the perfect wedding." He tilted his head and smiled softly. "The spring equinox? We'll do it the proper witch way."

"You mean that?" she whispered past her constricted throat.

It was no secret Coop had rejected magic at every turn during their odd mating dance. Until he'd come into his own powers and became comfortable with abilities being the norm, he'd been extremely wary of Summer and her family.

Not that she could blame him. At the time, her spells tended to backfire at every turn. She'd been afraid of her own gifts, of the sheer power she wielded, and used to pull back when she should've given it her all. Under Alastair's tutelage, she eventually learned to control what she had and give her abilities the free rein they needed to perform properly. Or mostly, anyway.

Coop waited expectantly, letting her make up her mind about the wedding venue and date.

"I think the spring equinox is perfect," she finally said.

"Not as perfect as you, sweetheart."

She pulled him down atop her, opening her legs to cradle his hips. "You say the sexiest things."

3

"*How* are Coop and Olivia?" Alastair asked as she approached.

Summer lowered her sunglasses to give her father a glare. "You'd better not have been spying!"

His rare bark of laughter boomed out. "Not a chance. I know good and well what I'd have seen if I did. There isn't enough eye bleach to wipe away the sight of Cooper's bare ass."

"I quite like his ass," she said cheekily, giving her father a wide grin as she settled back into a lounger. Seriously, the great Alastair Thorne using the term *eye bleach* tickled her funny bone. "Where's Mama? I thought she'd be here with you."

"She's with your sisters, getting us another drink, just there." With a tilt of his chin, he gestured to the poolside bar, where Aurora laughed with Autumn and Winnie. At a table not far from the others, Spring had settled on Knox's lap with one arm slung around his neck, grinning at something their other sister, Holly, appeared to be saying.

"Your mother is *still* trying to find some frou-frou concoction I might consume." Alastair sighed heavily. "It's like she doesn't know me at all."

"Mama is nothing if not optimistic. And don't worry. I'll drink whatever you don't want."

"You're a team player, my dear."

Summer's laughter died as he cocked his head to the side and studied her.

"What aren't you telling me, child?"

"Nothing?"

His lips twitched, and his eyes crinkled in amusement, but he remained silent, waiting for her to crack.

"Coop proposed."

"And still, there's no engagement ring on your finger. Miracles do happen."

She snorted in response to his sarcastic comment, knowing very well he'd probably had a hand in pairing them up, just as he had her sisters and their mates. Yet she couldn't quite figure out how he'd done it, and Alastair Thorne wasn't anywhere close to an open book, preferring to keep his wily methods to himself.

"Well, *no*, there isn't an engagement ring *yet*, but he gave me something much better." Sitting forward, Summer lifted the chain to show her father the locket. "It was his grandmother's."

Aurora arrived in time to hear Summer's reply.

"She was a lovely woman. I'm not sure if you remember her, dear, but she always made you a lemon loaf because it was your favorite."

"For me?" She was surprised by this turn in the conversation. It blew her mind that Coop's gran had specifically catered to *her* likes and dislikes. "I thought Miss Marina made it for everyone and I got the benefit of her culinary skills."

Her father chuckled. "Marina was a character."

"And she always spoiled you and your brother terribly, darling," Aurora replied with a grin.

"That she did. Most likely because we didn't terrorize her beloved Tristan like his siblings did." Alastair's smile was slightly sad in remembering the past. "You wouldn't know it, child, but once upon a time, Zane's father was the silent, studious one. He and Preston were bosom buddies and shared a love of antiquities."

"Quiet?" Her mother frowned as she handed Alastair a drink. "Why don't I remember him that way? He always seemed to be the life of the party."

"Yes, *after* college." He grimaced after taking a sip of his umbrella drink. "Not a winner, my love."

Summer readily accepted it when he handed it off to her. Taking a sip, she grinned. Piña coladas were never going to be a favorite of her father. "You should try a lemon-drop martini next time, Mama." Mainly, she'd said it because lemon was her favorite, and if she were going to get lit drinking her dad's rejects, she intended them to be ones she at least liked. "Please continue with the story, Dad."

"Right. As a child, Tristan lived in the shadow of Phillip and Marianne. Phillip mellowed after meeting and marrying Kiera, but as you know, their sister Marianne went the opposite direction."

Aurora shuddered and met Alastair's sympathetic gaze. "Evil minger is what I'd call her."

"That, too." He looked toward Knox and Spring. Both had been scarred by Marianne's single-minded devotion to her lover, Robert Knox, and the Thornes' longtime enemy, Zhu Lin.

"Thank the Goddess she's dead." Summer held up her piña colada and silently toasted Isis for gifting Knox the magical power and emotional strength to do what was necessary when it came to his mother and father.

"When Marianne ran off with Robert, Tristan was free to be himself. He came out of his shell, married Glory Ashbrooke, and had Zane." Alastair shrugged.

To him, it was the end of the story.

For Summer, it raised more questions, but there would always be time for things like that later. She was on vacation with her loved ones, life had reached a level of calm new to the Thornes, and she had an announcement to make.

After another sip of her drink, she cleared her throat. "Coop and I are getting married."

Her mother patted her arm. "We know, dear."

"No. We set a date. The spring equinox—at Thorne Manor." Holding her breath, she watched them both register her news, not failing to note her father's self-satisfied smile. Yep. He'd definitely had a hand in fixing them up.

"I think that's a fine idea, child," he told her.

"I thought you didn't necessarily care for Coop," she taunted, carefully gauging his response.

"I like him well enough… now. The boy had some growing up to do." Glancing around in what Summer assumed was his way of making sure the coast was clear, he conjured a drink that, based on the color, had to be his standard Glenfiddich.

"He was a grown man," Summer said dryly. "But I understand your reasoning. Besides, he's a great father."

"That's open for debate." He raised an arrogant brow when she smacked his arm. "The man has some cockamamie idea about encouraging Olivia to go through life suppressing her gifts. She's a *Thorne!*"

With a shared look of amusement and a hearty laugh, Summer and her mother shook their heads in unison.

"Oh, Dad."

Alastair grinned behind a sip of his scotch. After taking care to set the tumbler on the patio table, he uncrossed his ankles, placed his feet on the deck, and leaned forward. "Am I to assume you want Preston to walk you down the aisle?"

For someone who always held his cards to his chest, Alastair was as transparent as Saran Wrap.

"Actually, I want you both to, if you're okay to share the duty."

Again, she held her breath, awaiting his response. Her comment hadn't been to insult Alastair, but she'd grown up believing Preston was her father, and in every sense of the word, he'd been the perfect daddy to the insecure little girl she'd been. Summer didn't want to exclude him from the ceremony.

"I think that's a fine idea," Alastair said gruffly as he reached for her hand. "I know he'll be as honored as I am." With a quick squeeze of her fingers, he released her. "Who do you have in mind to officiate?"

"I hadn't gotten that far. Someone from the Witches' Council to make it official, I suppose."

"I know either Georgie Sipanil or Damian Dethridge would be willing."

"I don't know Miss Georgie as well as the rest of you, but I'd love it if Damian would."

"I'll give him a call." Alastair nodded as if it was a done deal. "You may need to make Sabrina one of your flower girls. That child won't take no for an answer."

Summer laughed. "She and Chloe can share the job as long as their parents are cool with it." The girls had become good friends over the last year, with Chloe teleporting to the Dethridge estate in England to have sleepovers with Damian's daughter, Sabrina. The two were thick as thieves and would get a kick out of being flower girls.

"And Olivia?" Aurora asked.

"She's too little, but I'm sure she'll be happy to sit with you and Dad." Summer cast him a side glance. "His little poopie-doop."

He groaned. "You were spying!"

"Of course we were, darling," her mother said as she ran her fingers through his hair, rumpling the thick mass and making him look more approachable. "It's like you don't know me at all."

He laughed and drew her down into his lap. "You are going to make a mighty hot mother of the bride."

"Ugh!" Summer stood up and grabbed the empty cups. "Try not to use words like *hot* in relation to Mama, okay?"

"Why? She's *totally* hot," he deadpanned. The twinkle in his eye gave him away, and they all laughed.

"Yeah, on that note, I'm going to return these to the bar and leave you two lovebirds alone to plot whatever it is you have in mind."

"You know me too well, child."

Summer kissed his cheek. "I love you, Dad. And thank you."

4

_S_ummer had just stepped from the shower when a knock sounded on her stateroom door. Going with the old tried-and-true witch way, she snapped her fingers to dry off and clothe herself. As she reached for the knob, the door burst open, knocking her on her butt.

"Fuck!"

A tiny squeak was quickly followed by an overly loud squawk as first one fellow cruiser, then another ran by the door opening, followed closely by a nest of mice. Multiple screams sounded in the hallway, and harried-looking crew members ran this way and that as they tried to calm passengers and collect rodents at the same time.

"Summer Thorne strikes again."

She glanced up at the auburn-haired sex kitten with her daisy-yellow bikini top and leopard sarong.

"Shut it, Tums. That's on you for your dam—uh, darn impatience." Summer accepted her older sister's hand up and dusted off the seat of her white capris. "You couldn't wait two more seconds for me to open the door?"

"Not when I've heard that you set a date for your wedding, I can't." Her sister's tone was drier than desert sand. "I'm hurt I wasn't the first to know."

"I felt I owed that to Mama and my dad. You were next after my shower."

Autumn's warm amber gaze swept her face, looking for any signs of deceit. Summer could've told her she'd never find any. Keeping secrets was next to impossible for her. For any of them, really. Such was the curse of a close-knit family.

Speaking of curses...

"We have to gather the mice, or we are going to have a major incident at sea."

Laughing, Autumn leaned back to check the hallway. "There had to be a lot of emotion behind that 'fuck' to have that many of the little buggers running around."

"You surprised me, and landing on my a—butt didn't exactly feel great."

"Well, do your little hocus-pocus and relocate them. I'll wipe the minds of everyone in the vicinity."

"If you weren't the cause of this, I'd say you're a lifesaver."

"Pfft." Her sister started to step into the hall, then

quickly turned back. "But I want to hear all about the proposal and the plans you've made so far when I get back. Deal?"

"You can't wait until lunch in"—Summer checked her smartwatch—"ten minutes?"

"No."

With that, Autumn sashayed out the door and lifted her arms. The last Summer saw before the door slammed shut was the swirling of her sister's fingers and a gray mist filling the air behind her.

Oh, to have Autumn's effortless talents.

"Goddess, hear my plea; assist me in this time of need. I ask you bring all those rodents back to me."

Squeaks and scratches sounded at the door, and one particularly gruff voice said, "Hurry the hell up, woman! The natives are restless, and one guy's looking a little like he wants to roast us over a spit."

After a deep, cleansing breath, she opened the door to the hundred or so mice loitering there.

Looking both ways down the hallway and pretending horror when she caught another passenger's panicked eye, Summer stepped backward into her room and gestured for the furry beasties to join her.

"Hurry up," she hissed.

Mice, like people, came in all shapes and sizes. And like everyday humans, they all had differing personalities, from hyper to lackadaisical. One particularly chubby mouse was eyeing the service tray outside the door of the adjoining room.

"Psst!"

He barely spared her a glance.

"*Psst!* Hey, buddy!"

Glancing left and right, he looked at her in question over his shoulder.

"Get a move on, or you're going to be caught and thrown to the fishes."

It didn't escape her notice that she sounded remarkably like her familiar, Saul, with his Godfather attitude. The little dude must be rubbing off on her. But if he were here, he'd definitely have these mice in line.

"Yancy, shake a freaking leg," came a gravelly voice next to her bare foot.

Yancy grabbed what he could of the remaining English muffin and hauled butt into her room. Summer closed the door in the face of a guy whose eye she happened to catch in the hallway. And she was certain he'd noticed her floor was littered with furry, chattering creatures, both big and small.

"Goddess, help me," she muttered.

Turning to look down at the expectant faces of her miniature visitors, she grimaced. "Okay, I'm going to need you to separate into groups. Starting with the southern states to the right and the northern states to the left. Those of you from the islands, you stay in the center."

Someone pounded on the door.

"Quickly," she urged on a whisper. Raising her voice, she called out, "One second!"

It took less than one minute of chaos, but the mice were grouped by region, then state or province. The door pounding continued as, one by one, she tapped into the mental picture the individual mouse gave her to send him home. When everyone was gone but Yancy and Clancy—that's what her grumbly assistant assured her his name was as she stared at him in disbelief—she shooed them into the bathroom and told them to hide under the towel she'd dumped on the floor.

After fluffing her hair and smoothing down her peasant top, she opened the door to see her annoying, bug-eyed fellow passenger.

He didn't bother to speak but charged into the room as if looking for evidence of her involvement in the mice-capades. The guy wouldn't be *wrong*, per se, but Summer liked to think she was getting the hang of cover-ups by now.

Hands behind her to keep the door propped open, she rocked back on her heels and surveyed the room with a keen eye for detail. She noticed some crumbs off to one side of the bed—thanks to Yancy—but wasn't too worried. Anyone would assume she was a slob, same with the towel on the bathroom floor. She just hoped this guy didn't feel the need to stomp over and pick it up in his quest for rodents.

"May I help you?"

"What did you do with them?"

Yep, he hadn't failed to notice the migration of mice into her stateroom. Heaving an internal sigh, she touched the tanzanite bracelet on her arm and mentally called her father. Ten seconds later, as she was still trying to come up with a legitimate excuse for what he'd seen, the lights in the hall flickered and the air grew heavy. Her father appeared and entered the fray.

"May I help you?" Alastair's sharp tone brought the passenger's head around.

"This chick is hiding a shit-load of mice here in her stateroom."

Dark-blond brows shot skyward, and a forbidding expression settled on Alastair's visage. "*Chick?* Don't you mean *lovely young woman?*"

Summer's not-so-bright visitor shook his head. "There's mice, man. Bunches of them! If my wife sees them, she's going to want to fly home when we dock in Barbados. Do you know how much a flight from Barbados to Michigan is?"

"Mice?" Alastair's tone dripped disbelief, and Summer was reminded what a consummate actor the man was. Hollywood had nothing on him, and her father had definitely missed his calling. "How many mice?" Alastair asked.

"Hundreds, man! Hundreds!" the guy practically

shouted, arms wildly flailing about. He was charging for the bathroom when Summer stepped in his path.

"Look, Mr...." She waited for him to fill in the blank, and when he didn't, she shrugged. "Look, sir, I don't know what you *think* you saw, but there's no way I'd be able to get that many rodents on board the ship without someone discovering them." Taking a page from her father's script, Summer mock shuddered. "And why would I want to?"

For a brief instant, the man looked uncertain, then firm resolve settled on his features, and he shook his head. "I saw them!"

Autumn sauntered into the room, took one look at the frantic passenger, and groaned. "I can't leave you alone for two minutes," she muttered. Raising her voice, she said, "Beat it, dude. My sister and I have a wedding to discuss."

Once again, the guy appeared unsure of himself. "But... I mean, I... that's to say..."

"Clearly, you can see there aren't hundreds of mice in this stateroom," Alastair said, effectively cutting off what would've been the man's full-blown babble. "I doubt there are any at all, really," her father continued with a sharp look in her direction.

From behind the guy's back, she shrugged and held up two fingers.

Alastair's mouth tightened, but he remained firm in his resolve to send the half-hysterical man on his way. "I suggest you go back to your room, call room service, and have them bring you a nice meal with a Merlot." He produced a hundred-dollar bill and shoved it into the man's pudgy hand. "By the time you reach the bottom of the bottle, all this will have been a terrible dream, and you'll feel generous enough to give this to the room attendant."

The air conditioner kicked up, and with it came the aroma of a perfectly seared steak and steamed vegetables, followed a moment later by the scent of chocolate cake. A suggestive spell, woven by her father to distract the man, but even Summer began to crave the foods he suggested. The mighty Thorne made spell casting look easy-peasy. However, it was anything but. Suggestion spells took considerable talent.

After the door closed, Autumn began to laugh. Not just a lighthearted giggle, but breath-stealing guffaws that doubled her over. Summer joined in. Gone were the days of embarrassment over her wonky magic.

"If you two are done, lunch is in five." Alastair kissed Summer's temple to show he wasn't truly upset and promptly disappeared.

"Think anyone caught him teleporting into the hallway?" her sister asked when she could catch her breath. "The whole light-flickering scene was straight out of the Titanic movie."

"Right? I thought that guy was going to stroke out." Their conversation dissolved into more laughter. This was what Summer had missed the most when she and her siblings had all formed relationships and moved out of the manor, the shared confidences and endless humor.

Out of the blue, Autumn hugged her as if she sensed Summer's thoughts. And perhaps she had. Autumn was *hella* intuitive and an expert at human behavior. It's what made her a formidable businesswoman.

"I love you, Tums," Summer said.

"Ditto, sis. Now, tell me all about Coop's second proposal and what plans you've thought up."

"We only have three more minutes until we have to join the others."

"Meh. They'll wait. I mean, seriously, where are they going? We're on an ocean liner, cruising the Caribbean." The spark of amusement was so similar to Alastair's earlier that Summer had to smile. They both knew damned well her family could disappear with a mere thought and blink of an eye.

"We decided on the spring equinox, and now we only have less than two months to pull this together. I'm worried I can't arrange it in time with work, a baby, and everything else."

"Leave it to Mama and me. We'll get it done. I promise your ceremony will eclipse mine in every way."

"That's not what I want, Tums. I..." The thing was, she didn't know what she wanted other than to be married to Coop. To finally commit to him as he intended to commit to her—with their whole hearts and souls.

"We're witches, Summer. We've got this in the bag, babe."

5

"Don't take this the wrong way, but I hate wedding planning." Summer flopped back on the bed, arms spread wide, angsty expression firmly in place. "Why does it have to be so damned hard to make a decision?"

Seeing her stressed to the extent she was, bothered Coop. He tugged her into a sitting position and pulled her into the circle of his arms. "What can I do to help?"

"You already have, just by being here."

"Summer."

"It's the details. We're witches. We should be able to conjure whatever we want, but for some reason, my mother feels it's important to do this the old-fashioned mortal way. No magic." His soon-to-be wife blew out a breath and groaned.

"There was a time you'd have wanted to do it the old-fashioned mortal way. You were afraid of your abilities," he said, reminding her of when her power had been wonky. If it hadn't been for her ill-timed, mismanaged magic, she and Coop probably wouldn't be a couple. "I believe, to a degree, you still are. Perhaps your mother feels you'd be more invested in the wedding if you took part instead of allowing Autumn to conjure everything."

Summer pulled away to study his face. "Are you upset that Autumn wants to take charge?"

"Not really, but this entire ceremony should be what *you* want, not what your sister feels is appropriate."

"She probably knows me better than I know myself," Summer said as she settled back into the embrace.

"No, she doesn't. She knows the things about you that you allow others to see. Deep down, where it counts, you hide away." He held up his hands when she jerked back to protest. "Not that it's a bad thing, sweetheart. But you've kept your insecurities hidden for a long time, never allowing those close to you to see your inner turmoil."

The pique disappeared from her visage, and a sheepish expression took the place of her irritation. "You're right. I was a bundle of insecurity."

"With Alastair's help, you've been able to explore your magic. And because you've gained confidence, you were able to build on it and become formidable in your own right. That's progress, and you should be proud of all you've accomplished."

"I love you, Coop. And I am. Proud, that is." She rose to her feet and stood between his spread legs to toy with the buttons of his uniform shirt. "Your support and acceptance of our gifts have made all the difference."

"There was a time when the idea of magic almost made me shit my pants. When you froze me in place—more than once!—I thought I was having a fucking stroke. It didn't warm my heart or endear me to the process in the least little bit."

She giggled. "But now look at you! You're an old pro, taking to magic like a duck to water."

"Mmhmm." His tone was drier than dirt, and it appeared to tickle her funny bone because she laughed. He stroked her cheek. "There. That's the look I wish I could see all the time. Your happiness is what I live for."

"Ugh." With a roll of her eyes, she slapped his chest. "Corny much?"

Coop hooked an arm around her waist and drew her up flush against him. "Hush, you! I can wax poetic with the best of them."

"Stick with sheriffing, Sheriff."

With a low growl, he captured her mouth, savoring the rich sweetness of whatever chocolate she'd consumed earlier as he tasted his fill. When they parted, the sparkle in her eyes partnered with her wide, appreciative grin.

"Or making love. You do that exceptionally well, too, Sheriff Carlyle."

Laughing, he pulled her atop him as he fell back on the bed. "I'm always happy to oblige, ma'am. Part of my duty to my community."

Summer poked his chest, and it was her turn to growl. "You'd better not be obliging others in your community. Not the way you *oblige* me, anyway."

"It's only you, sweetheart. You keep me active enough for all Leiper's Fork's residents combined."

Coop captured her hand and bit down gently on her finger, then sucked it into his mouth and drew it out slowly. Her expression turned decidedly interested as she watched the progress of her finger entering his mouth and withdrawing again under her own steam.

Real regret clouded her eyes. "I have to meet my mother for cake tasting in Franklin in less than thirty minutes. I don't have time for you to *oblige* me."

"I'll drive."

"I'm serious, Coop—"

"No, I mean, I'll drive to the cake shop, but I do like the way you think." He winked and rolled her onto her back to steal another kiss. Lungs straining and dick aching with need, he pulled away and sighed. "Tonight, we pick this conversation up again. Right here, in this spot."

"Agreed." She arched up and gave him a hard peck

on his lips. "It's a date. Now, take me to get cake, my love."

Hand in hand, they walked to Coop's service vehicle. After a quick call to Lil in dispatch, they were on the road to Franklin.

As the highway stretched in front of them and the Carlyle estate was in the review mirror, Summer turned slightly in her seat to study the profile of her fiancé and forever love. He was so strong, handsome, and capable, with a gooey center. Who knew? Certainly not her, not in the early days when he would decree this or that in regard to her sanctuary, like he was the King of America.

But underneath his gruff exterior and hard-as-nails attitude, Coop cared. Not just for her, but for people in general. He wanted to help. To keep them safe. And though it had taken a while for Summer to understand and accept, he'd only wanted to shut down her rescue operation to protect the residents of their town. Her especially. The reason was that he'd been worried her chimpanzee was unstable. Now, knowing Morty had a heart of gold and was unable to hurt a fly, Coop was more trusting of her small ape.

"You know you didn't have to take me to Franklin, Coop. I could've met my mother and father myself."

A quicksilver grimace crossed his face. "You didn't tell me Alastair was going to be there."

"Didn't I?"

"You know damned well you didn't. You said your mother."

Summer grinned as she faced forward. Yep, she'd omitted the fact her formidable father would be at the bakery, but when Coop thought about it longer, he'd realize Aurora didn't go anywhere without Alastair. Not after the love of her father's life had spent nearly two decades in a coma.

"Should we have brought Olivia? She'd have kept my dad occupied."

Coop grunted. "Maybe until she crapped her diaper. Then Alastair would've handed her back to me with some lecture on how to magically change the damned thing."

Biting back a laugh, Summer acknowledged to herself that Coop was correct. Alastair loved to torture him with the little things and about magical abilities in particular.

"Knox and Spring are always happy to take Ollie, sweetheart. You know that. I feel my cousin secretly wants babies but is afraid to mention it to his wife for fear she doesn't want them."

"Knox is afraid of Spring?" Summer smiled. "Just wait until I tell her."

"Don't you dare! He'll kill me, badge or no."

"Fine, but I dub thee Spoiler of Fun."

Coop's deep chuckle filled the cab. "You already did. Ages ago."

"For the record, Spring isn't against babies. She simply wants to enjoy alone time with Knox for a while longer. Preferably, she'd like to wait until thirty-three to get started, or so she said. That gives them another few years to be child-free and travel."

"Will it go against your sisterly code if I reveal it to him?"

"Nah. She'd probably tell him herself if he were brave enough to ask."

When they pulled up at the bakery in Franklin, Summer spotted her parents on the sidewalk in front of the shop. She paused to watch their interaction, marveling at how young they appeared and how in love they still were. As Aurora spoke, Alastair hyper focused on her. At that moment, she was his be-all, end-all, and he hung on every word as it fell from her lips. She, in turn, was animated, waving her hands in the air as she spoke. Deep and abiding love shone from the ice-blue eyes locked on her partner, and she threw back her head to laugh at some quip he uttered in response to whatever she'd just told him.

They existed in a world of their own, and yet, the instant Coop parked the SUV, Alastair raised his head and shot them a quick glance.

"How does he do that?" Coop shook his head. "It's like he knew we were here the entire time."

"Ask him. But I imagine he can feel the power of two witches."

"Hmm. Good point." Clasping hands, he

approached her parents and greeted them with his usual friendly but professional Sheriff nod.

Aurora was having none of his distant behavior, and she hugged him as if he were one of her own children, showering him with affection. "Cooper!"

"Good morning, Rorie. Thanks for doing this. Summer and I would still be wondering where to start with the wedding prep."

"Nonsense, dear. She's my daughter, and you're about to become my son. This is a mother's fondest wish."

"To plan a wedding?" Alastair asked, droll as fuck.

She elbowed him in the ribs. "To see her daughter happy." With a quick check of her watch, she ushered them inside. "Come. We have a short window until the next cake tasting. Carla was a love and worked us in as a favor to her mother."

"Who's her mother?" Summer asked.

"My old school friend, Cora Masters."

"Masters?" Alastair frowned. "Any relation to Draven Masters, the reluctant Guardian?"

"Distant cousins, I believe," Rorie replied with a thoughtful look. She shrugged and waved her hand. "We can ask her. But for right now, cake!"

6

The cake samples ranged from the traditional flavors—vanilla with buttercream, decadent chocolate, and strawberry—to a unique explosion of flavors for the more discerning palate.

"There has to be at least fifteen varieties here." To say Coop was surprised by the plethora of options, all handwritten so neatly on the placement cards, was to put it mildly. He could count on one hand the number of weddings he'd attended in his lifetime, and they were run-of-the-mill, basic vanilla cake with buttercream frosting. "I've never heard of half those flavors. Chocolate Chai? Honey Lavender?"

"Blackberry elder. Olive oil, rosemary, and thyme. Hazelnut pumpkin." Alastair shuddered noticeably. "As much as I hate to agree with Cooper, I believe some of these flavors are over the top."

"I never said they were over the top," Coop replied.

Sure, he'd thought it, but he hadn't said it aloud. It wouldn't do to look like a provincial, backwater Deputy Do-Right.

"You didn't have to. I felt your revulsion, son."

"Fine. But for Summer's sake, I'm not ruling anything out." He paused and eyed the label for the olive oil, rosemary, and thyme plate. "Except for that one," he said, pointing at the offending cake. "I can't imagine olive oil in a cake tastes all that great."

"Agreed," Rorie said with a light laugh. "While pies and breads may be savory, I think we all prefer a little sweetness in our cake."

Aurora had the type of laugh that drew a person in. Sometimes verging on naughty and hinting at reckless depths, and at other times, bubbly and bright, making the listener want to take part in whatever she found amusing.

Alastair leaned in close, speaking in a low voice for only Coop's hearing. "Suck up."

As Coop sputtered his indignation, Alastair smirked and approached Summer. "Would you like to test all the samples, my dear child, or would you prefer to narrow it down to five to try?"

"Nice try, Dad. But no, we're sampling them all. Even the olive-oil cake." Coop pretended to gag for her amusement, and she glared her response. "All of them, Coop."

"Yes, dear," he said, mocking her with a wide flare of his eyes and a contrite expression.

As she turned toward the table, he caught sight of her grin. Although it was never far from the surface, his unadulterated love for her boiled up and over, and he experienced a moment of awe that she chose him to love in return. She'd picked him and never wavered, even when he'd been a jerk with his head stuck so far up his ass that he couldn't see daylight. And despite the fact he hadn't deserved it, she gave him chance after chance whenever his fear got the better of him or he rejected the idea of magic.

Coop dutifully sampled cakes—olive oil and all— then weighed in with his opinion as Summer jotted notes. After removing the phone from her hand, he pushed a plate toward her.

"Your turn. I'm not the only one involved in this wedding, sweetheart."

"What's your favorite?" she asked, blissfully ignoring the fact he'd attempted to include her.

"What's *your* favorite?" he countered.

When she glanced up from the notes she'd been scribbling, understanding dawned on her beloved face, and she wrinkled her nose as she grimaced. "Yeah, sorry. I'll try some."

He frowned at her lack of enthusiasm. "Summer, are you feeling okay?"

"A little nauseous, truth be told. It's probably the stress of the planning."

Alastair's deep chuckle caught their notice, and the

wry amusement on his face as he watched them told Coop they were missing something deeper.

"Care to enlighten the rest of us?" Coop asked testily. Had Summer's condition been serious, her father wouldn't have been nonchalant about it. The only reason he'd find anything funny was if the two of them were missing the point altogether.

Nausea.

An alarm went off in Coop's head, and he whipped around to stare at Summer. "You're pregnant."

"What? No! I—" She paled, placed a hand on her stomach, and looked back at her father for confirmation. If she was carrying another soul, her energy signature would be double.

Sure enough, Alastair grinned. "Princess Poopie Pants will have a baby brother or sister to spoil by the end of the year."

"Ohmygoddess!"

Summer looked ready to faint. Shoving back his chair, Coop rushed to assist her.

"Another baby? Coop, we can barely keep up with Olivia. Between my practice, the sanctuary, and family life, I'm already running on empty," she cried tearfully.

For some time, he had been toying with the idea of retiring from the force. Of handing the reins to his next in line so he could ease Summer's burden by taking over her sanctuary and caring for Olivia during the day. The knowledge of another bundle of joy arriving before they'd expected it now cemented his decision.

"I'm resigning as sheriff."

"Coop!"

"No, listen. I've been thinking about this for quite a while, and it feels right. It's time we stop popping back and forth and make our home in North Carolina."

"But you love being sheriff," she protested.

"I love you and our family more. That includes your zoo and our future son or daughter," he replied, overcome with tenderness for his wife. His voice wasn't quite steady when he said, "Nothing is as important as all of you."

With a soft sob, she wrapped her arms around his neck and buried her nose against his throat. Her hot tears dripped past the collar of his shirt, running down his skin until the material soaked up the moisture.

"Is that a yes?" he asked softly.

"I'd love that. Yes."

"It's settled, then. When we get home today, I'll put in my notice and start grooming my replacement."

"Oh, Coop."

"A baby," he murmured his wonder as he held her and stroked her silky hair. "We're going to be outnumbered in a few years if we keep this up."

She laughed as he'd intended her to. Drawing back, she smiled up at him. "I think it's time for you to learn how to magically change a diaper from my father."

When he groaned, they all laughed. "Fine, but then

I'm going to demand the Luscious Lemon wedding cake for our reception."

"Done."

***

TWO WEEKS LATER, Summer was lamenting her previously thin waistline. It seemed as if her belly, along with her new little peanut, had grown overnight. The dress she'd originally decided on felt too tight and constraining.

"I can't wear this," she grumbled to her sisters.

"You can." Autumn's firm tone got on Summer's last remaining nerve for the day.

"Fuc—"

Three of her four sisters stared in shock as the fourth laughingly slapped a hand over her mouth.

"None of that, or we'll be inundated with mice," Holly warned. "Oh, but of course, you're pregnant now, so the standard curse doesn't apply." Removing her hand, she grinned. "Swear away!"

"Damn straight!" Summer snapped, half expecting the follow-up sneeze. It didn't happen, and with her breath held, she waited to see if the local mouse population would make an appearance. When she didn't hear so much as a squeak, she sighed her relief.

"Okay, so about this dress..." Winnie positioned Summer in front of the mirror and took up residence behind her. Brow puckered, she nodded. "This isn't you, and it doesn't flow. You need something lighter. Filmier."

"What's wrong with the dress?" Autumn glared her displeasure.

"You picked it, sister," Spring said, not unkindly. "It's what *you* would wear, and perhaps what Summer would've worn prior to starting a family with Coop, but it doesn't capture the essence of who she is today."

Grudgingly, Autumn nodded. "Valid."

"I don't know what I want, but I know it's not something this tight." Summer shot an apologetic look at Autumn. "I'm sorry, Tums."

"Don't be. This is *your* wedding, and like Winnie said, it isn't you. If I'd have thought about it longer, I'd have realized it. But don't be afraid to speak up when it comes to everything else."

"I'm not. I won't. I'm..." Summer shrugged and plucked at the satiny material of the dress.

Spring captured her hands and clasped them between hers. "What's wrong?"

"Life has changed so much in such a short time. We were all together as a family unit, and now, we're paired off, with the majority of us as parents. I miss my sisters." Glancing up, she met their concerned gazes one by one. "I miss moments like these and times when we all sit around, eating Winnie's cinnamon rolls and discussing the idiot Carlyle boys."

With a wide grin and a wink, Autumn plopped down on the mattress. "Well, if it makes you feel any better, I still consider them all 'idiot Carlyle boys.' And I've no problem gossiping about them."

"But I want family functions where all our children grow up together. They deserve to have a solid family unit like we did."

Holly raised her hand. "Exception here."

"Yeah, but you're one of us *now*," Spring replied as she wrapped an arm around Holly's waist. "And that's never going to change."

"You're my favorite sister," Holly declared and rested her head on their youngest sibling's shoulder.

"Let's make a pact," Winnie suggested with an excited smile. "From this day forward, we will make the time to get together at least once per month for a family picnic. Husbands, children, and all. No exceptions."

"No exceptions," they all replied in unison.

"Mama's going to love that," Holly said with a soft smile. "Have you noticed how attentive she is since she returned to the living? Do you think she's trying to make up for the past?"

"She has nothing to make up for," Summer replied. "I can't say I wouldn't have done the same thing had it been Coop. I'd have followed him anywhere. Done anything."

"But at the expense of your children?"

They all faced Spring. Summer considered her question, weighing it in her mind. "Probably not. I can't imagine leaving Olivia with anyone else to raise."

"Don't judge her too harshly. She suffered enough because of her choices. The stasis stole a lot from her." Autumn cleared her throat and blinked her eyes, clearly affected by the conversation. "Yes, we have the right to be a little salty, but we didn't live her life. We don't know what trials she faced or how much they weighed into her decisions. She loved one man to distraction while being married to another, and all because she thought Alastair was dead." She looked at each of them in turn. "What would you have done for the love of your life if he returned after all those years?"

"None of us are in a position to judge, Tums, and we all love her." Summer stepped forward and hugged her. "What's going on with you? Why are you so adamant about this?"

"I'm not sure. I guess I just don't want her to feel like an outsider."

"She's not. We all love her."

"I know." Autumn gave Summer one last squeeze. "Now, let's conjure the dress of your dreams!"

"Quickly, before Mama drags me to a brick-and-mortar store to find another one."

7

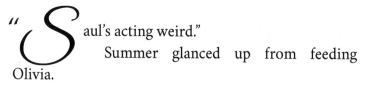

"*S*aul's acting weird."

Summer glanced up from feeding Olivia.

Coop stood with his hands on his hips and a grim expression on his face. It had been a week since he'd officially quit his job, and Summer suspected he was looking for problems to solve, as he was wont to do.

"How so?" she asked, turning back to spoon mashed potatoes into her daughter's rapidly closing mouth. When Olivia spit them out onto the high chair's tray, Summer sighed tiredly. The little gremlin refused to eat these days unless she could feed herself.

Giving up, Summer handed over the spoon and silently prayed it wouldn't turn into a potato rain shower in their kitchen. Olivia had learned her latest trick of flicking food from her mischievous cousin, Jolly. It was all fun and games until Summer found dried guck on the cabinets that she'd happened to miss the first time.

"No flinging food," she warned her daughter. When Olivia grinned evilly, Summer narrowed her eyes. "I mean it, you little monster."

They had a stare-off for another thirty seconds before Olivia shrugged a shoulder, Autumn-style, and crammed a fistful of potatoes in her mouth with one hand, then followed it up with a spoonful from the other. Satisfied she could turn away, Summer faced Coop. He was resting back against the counter, arms folded over his chest and ankles crossed. An amused grin graced his face.

Joining him by the sink, she lowered her voice to say, "It's not funny. Your daughter is a brat. But that's on you, Nanny Man. Anyway, what makes you think Saul is acting weird?"

"He's being sketchy."

"He's always sketchy. He's Saul."

"Well, sketchier than normal."

With an eye roll that almost revealed her brain matter, Summer began putting their leftovers into containers. "What *specifically* has Saul done, Coop?"

"Nothing."

"Then don't worry about him. He's probably organizing his squirrel mafia for some unknown reason."

"There!" Coop pointed at her. "That's what I'm talking about. Why would he need to organize his squirrel mafia?"

"He's Saul."

"You keep saying that, and it doesn't make me feel any better. I sleep with one eye open since your cruise. That thug terrifies me."

She giggled, and the sound was echoed by Olivia, who watched them with rapt attention.

"Squir-bits!" Ollie shouted, banging on her tray. "Squir-bits! Squir-bits!"

"Christ, not that again," Coop muttered as he rubbed the spot between his brows. In an instant, his head shot up, and he stared at Summer in horror. "You don't think that's it, do you? Did he get that rabbit pregnant?"

"Coop, listen to yourself." She couldn't prevent another laugh. "Squirrels and rabbits can't breed."

"Tell *him* that!"

"I have!" She bit the inside of her cheek to contain her amusement. When she was able to talk again with a straight face, she said, "He told me he could love her from afar."

"Ohdeargawd!"

"Give him another month, and he'll have fallen for someone else."

"Or something," Coop muttered in disgust. He hugged her from behind and kissed her neck. "So you don't think something's up with him?"

"Probably nothing serious."

"Fine. But if shit hits the fan, it's on you."

"Deal. Now go pry the potatoes from your little

princess's fingers. She's getting ready to decorate the wall."

Quick to react, Coop swept Olivia up in his arms and peppered her face with kisses, much to their daughter's squealed delight. Love filled Summer's heart to overflowing as she watched father and child play. Placing her hand on her abdomen, she sighed her contentment. Soon, he'd have another one to spoil. Who knew the tough-as-nails, retired sheriff of Leiper's Fork would be such an adoring dad?

"I love you," Summer blurted out.

Surprise lit his face as he turned from blowing raspberries on Olivia's exposed belly, and when his gaze locked with Summer's, his expression softened. "I love you, too, sweetheart."

"And I'll keep an eye on Saul. We don't want him to mess anything up between now and our wedding."

"Thanks." Coop grinned, and she felt it to her toes.

Coop had been right.

Saul was up to something.

Summer could feel the disturbance in the force. As her familiar, Saul shared an almost spiritual-like link with her, and right now, his energy was sketchy as fuck.

"What's going on, Saul?" she asked when she'd cornered him in the large-animal barn.

"Whaddya mean?"

He was the poster child for guilty expressions everywhere.

"Saul." Her tone warned him she wasn't messing around and answers were required.

Still, he backpedaled. "Yeah, I don't know why da fuck you're singling me out. Like I've got anything to hide. This is a setup from that mudderfuc—"

"Saul! If you continue to call Coop names, I swear you're going to be out on your furry butt."

Hurt flashed in his eyes, and Summer felt it in her soul. Poor Saul was hard on the outside, but inside, he was a marshmallow, especially when it counted. Or at least he was regarding her and Olivia. He still hadn't warmed to Coop.

Summer scooped Saul up and rubbed her cheek against the top of his fluffy head. "You know I adore you, right? But you have to make nice with Coop. I love him, and he's not going anywhere. He's my forever love and the father of my children." She met his wide topaz eyes. "Please, Saul. Make nice."

"Fine." Though his tone was gruff and his expression surly, Saul's loving vibe trumped them.

"Thank you." With a tender kiss on his forehead, she released him and smiled as he scampered off. "I'm on to you, little man," she murmured. "If you're up to something, I'll figure it out."

"Sounds ominous."

Summer whirled to face the entrance of the barn,

where Knox Carlyle stood, grinning at her. Placing a hand on the area over her heart, she blew out a breath. "Dude. You scared the bejeezus out of me."

"I thought you and Coop were expecting me." He sauntered to her and gave her a tight hug. "Congrats on the pregnancy. Spring told me. And Coop informed me what you said about Spring's desire to wait a few more years."

"I find it difficult to believe you're afraid of my sister," Summer replied dryly.

"Just the dirt she likes to magically put in my mouth when I tick her off."

They shared a laugh and another hug. Keeping her arm around his waist, they strolled toward the house. "Did Coop tell you why he called you to come by?"

"Something about rings?"

"We'd like for you to help us design ours."

Knox shook his head. "Design? I'm no jeweler, babe."

"Well, make them, really. We have a general idea in mind."

"Okay. Do you have a sketch?"

"I do. Is there any metal you can't work with?"

"No. Whatever you require, I can mold to your design."

Summer smiled up at him. "Thank you. More than anything else, I want these rings to be perfect."

"I'll try my best."

"I know." She gave him a light squeeze around his

middle, then released him to open the door. "Come on, let me show you what we've come up with."

About twenty minutes later, they'd decided on the precious metal from a suggestion Knox had made.

"I don't understand how platinum can harness the power of the moon," Coop said. "Does it really matter if it's from some sacred spot in... where did you say?"

"Australia. And yes." Knox leaned back in his seat and crossed his arms. "At the peak of the lunar cycle."

"I think it's sweet that you want to give us that added blessing," Summer said as she set a mug of coffee down. As she placed a cup in front of Coop, she gave him a stern warning look. "And you do, too."

He dragged her onto his lap and stole a kiss. "And I do, too."

She beamed her happiness.

"Man, are you whipped," Knox teased with a laugh. "Who would've thought the day would come when hardass Cooper Carlyle would become malleable and agreeable?"

"Shut it," Coop growled. But there was no real heat in his comment. In fact, he looked smug and exceedingly content.

Knox downed the last of his drink and rose. "Okay, full moon is tomorrow night. I'll pop down under and get what I need to create your rings." He picked up the drawings. "This the final design, or do you want to work on it more?"

Heart thudding, Summer gazed up at him, feeling

worried she'd somehow screwed up. "Is it a sucky design?"

Expression indulgent and kind, he shook his head. "It's beautiful. I'm just making sure so I can create exactly what you want. If you're done with the details, I'll take these sketches. If you're not, I'll come back for them."

She accepted the drawings and studied them for a full minute before holding them up for Coop. "What do you think?"

"I'm happy with what we've come up with. You?"

Slowly, she nodded, gaining confidence in her decision. "I am."

"Then give the sketches to Knox and let him work his personal magic."

After accepting them, Knox dropped a kiss on her cheek. "They're perfect, Summer. Don't worry. I'll have the finished rings for you in a few days, okay?"

"Thank you, Knox. It means more to us than you can possibly know."

Summer was still sitting on Coop's lap a few minutes later, thinking about what the finished product might look like, when his lips brushed her neck.

"Don't stress, sweetheart. I know my cousin. He's a perfectionist, and our rings will be incredible."

"You think?"

"I know," he said confidently.

Leaning back, she tilted her neck to allow him

better access. "You know, it's Saturday. The office is closed, and Olivia's sleeping."

"Mmm, you don't say," he murmured as he pressed light kisses along the column of her throat. Pausing at the sensitive spot beneath her ear, he scraped her skin with his teeth. "What did you have in mind?"

So there wasn't any mistake, she moved his hand from her waist to her breast. "Oh, I don't know. Maybe a *nap*."

"I love *napping* with you."

Laughing, she stood and dragged him to his feet. "Last one to the bed is a rotten egg."

"It's always a contest with you." He bent and tossed her over his shoulder. "Comfy? Not putting too much pressure on your belly?"

"All good, kind sir! Take me to bed."

With a light slap to her butt, he strode down the hallway.

8

*W*ith great care, Coop shifted Summer from his shoulder to his arms and laid her on their bed. He spared an extra moment to simply take in the beauty of her face as she gazed up at him, love shining in her eyes and transforming her visage from pretty to stunning.

"I'm the luckiest sonofabitch alive," he said gruffly. "I don't know what I did to deserve you, but I'm happy I did it."

Her already wide smile grew. "I'd say we were both lucky. Love isn't guaranteed in life, and for sure, it's important to recognize and nurture it when it comes our way."

"Truer words were never spoken."

Taking his time, he reached a hand over his shoulder and grabbed a handful of his shirt, drawing it over his head. With a flick of his wrist, he sent it sailing toward the chair in the corner.

"I love when you do that," Summer said with a girly sigh.

He laughed because she was always quick to tell him so every time he undressed, and if Coop could give her a small thrill by stripping the way she liked, he would. With great deliberation, he placed his hands on the waistband of his jeans.

"What about this?" Taking his time, he unbuttoned his pants and eased the zipper down with maddening slowness.

Her expression turned sly. "Hmm. Well, I don't know. What do you think when I do this?" Lifting her hips, she copied his move by unbuttoning and unzipping her pants, taking twice as long to do it.

When she stopped, her pink lace panties were visible in the V of the opening.

Coop's mouth watered.

"I took my shirt off first," he reminded her as he lazily shucked his jeans and boxer briefs. "You're not keeping up."

"Good point." Shifting to a sitting position, she inched her shirt up over the beginning of her baby bump, then her ribs, and finally over her chest to reveal the lacy bra that was the mate to her underwear.

He grinned his appreciation and, with his fingertips,

followed the path the hem of her shirt had traveled until he cupped the fullness of her breast. "And of course, since I don't wear a bra, this one is going to have to go. *Stat*."

"What will you give me in return?"

"Whatever the fuck you want."

She laughed at his emphatic response and unclipped her bra, sending it sailing toward his shirt right before she shimmied out of her underwear. "Better?"

"Much!"

Straddling him, she ran her hands over the planes of his chest, then lower, over his abdomen. Balancing herself with one hand on the bed, she gripped his dick in her other. He closed his eyes as she stroked him, happy to let her take the lead in their lovemaking.

When she stopped caressing him, Coop opened his eyes to stare up at her. The lustful look on her face made him harder than all the practiced ministrations of her hand ever could. Arching up, he covered her mouth with his, slipping his tongue inside to steal the necessary taste of her. As their kiss grew heated, he imagined he could taste her love and the future promise of all their tomorrows.

He trailed his hands up her rib cage and cupped the fullness of her breasts, smiling as she moaned.

With his thumbs, he toyed with her hardened nipples, then lightly rolled them between his fingers, tugging gently as he would if he were sucking them.

Again, she moaned.

Coop pressed her back with one hand, bringing her chest within tasting distance. As he drew her down farther, he opened his mouth and took one tight nipple into his mouth, groaning his own pleasure when her legs tightened around his hips in response.

He was certain he could spend hours tasting her skin, suckling her breasts, touching her most private areas, all just to elicit her sexy response and drive her mad with desire, as she always seemed to drive him crazy.

Impatiently, she gripped his hair and tugged him away from her chest, then she kissed him fully as she reached for his dick and positioned it at her opening.

"Slow down, sweetheart. We have time for that."

"I want you in me. Now. I'm on fire for you, Coop."

"Don't take this the wrong way, but I fucking love when you're pregnant. When those pregnancy hormones fire up... Ah!" He gasped as she sheathed him in her tight, hot passage. "Jesus, Summer!"

Buried deep inside her was as close to heaven as Coop had ever been, and he never wanted to leave the bed. After a long, delicious moment of her tightening the walls of her vagina around him, he gave in to her unrelenting demand and touched her clit with his thumb, pressing and circling as she panted her need. She surged upward and ground against the palm of his hand before seating herself on his cock again.

He cried out his pleasure as she rocked over him, drawing herself away only to crash back down and grind her hips against his. Gripping her waist, he rocked up against her, helping her develop a rhythm to satisfy them both.

The pressure built, and just when his balls began to tighten, he lifted her off him and lowered her onto her back.

"What the fuck are you doing?"

"Too quick," he panted. "I want this to last."

"Maybe I like it quick," she grumbled.

With a laugh, he sat back on his heels. "I guarantee you'll like this so much more."

"I'd better," she warned.

With a confident smirk, he spread her legs wide and used the head of his penis to caress her folds, running the tip up and down until her body wept with her hunger for him. Then Coop bent and touched his tongue to her, sweeping it along her opening and stopping only when he reached her clit. When she arched into him, he sucked on the tiny bud, hard, and inserted two fingers into her.

She cried out in her pleasure, greedy for more.

And he gave it to her. Fingers, tongue, penis, whatever she demanded in every way she demanded it. Her mindless cries urged him on, as did her arching body. She met each of his forceful thrusts with a sobbing plea for more, making him feel like a god as he pleasured her.

He smoothed the sweat-dampened hair back from her flushed face as he memorized her every wanton expression. With each pump of his hips, he felt a deep satisfaction that he could make her experience such ecstasy.

"Come for me, sweetheart. Scream for me." He pistoned his hips to emphasize each word, building his own orgasm just as hers built. When her walls contracted around him, he allowed himself to let go, gasping out her name as his release rocked him and her body sucked his dry.

And that second was always his favorite. The one where he crested the wave with her and rode it all the way home.

FROM HER POSITION BENEATH COOP, Summer stretched her arms over her head and yawned. "Best nap ever!"

His deep chuckle resonated inside her chest, causing a tickling sensation. Running her hands down the smooth skin of his back, she settled them over his generously muscled ass and squeezed.

"Goddess, you're good at that."

"I could say the same about you, sweetheart."

Coop dropped a kiss on her lips and started to roll, but she held him in place.

"I'm not done with you yet," she said. "I'm going to need more. Much more."

His brows shot up even as his penis twitched against her belly, hardening inch by delicious inch.

"Far be it for me to deny you, but what if our baby comes out with a dent in his head?"

She laughed. "Olivia didn't, and you know how insatiable I was then."

"True." Gathering up her hair from beneath her neck, he spread it out on the pillow around her, then he gazed down at her with all the brightness of the noonday sun. "There is nothing I would deny you, Summer. You know that, right?"

"Good. Because you know what I want," she said huskily.

He grinned, and she felt a rush of heat at the apex of her thighs. How the hell he made her wet with a grin, she'd never know, but the carnal look in his eyes only added to her desire. And when he slowly entered her, joining with her until she couldn't tell where her body ended and his began, she moaned her pleasure.

Coop took his time loving her, not rushing despite her urging. And as frustrated as she was, she appreciated his thoroughness that much more. When she was finally satiated, the baby monitor let her know Olivia was awake and ready to play.

"Ugh. Is it wrong to say I miss the days of single, childless adulthood? I mean, I wouldn't trade what we have for the world, but all my limbs are refusing to cooperate. I feel like I'm made of rubber," Summer complained.

"I've got this. Take a real nap, and I'll wake you in a few hours."

"You'd do that for me?"

"Anything, remember?"

"I adore you."

He laughed. "Good. Let's keep it that way." With a quick, affectionate kiss, he drew up his jeans and pulled a shirt over his head. "Get some rest. Dinner will be ready when you wake up."

As Summer listened to Coop talk to Olivia through the monitor, she smiled sleepily. The love he felt for their child was evident in his tone and teasing. Olivia's giggles were proof positive that she loved him just as much. How could she not? Coop was everything a father should be: attentive, caring, and protective.

Summer pressed her palms together. "Thank you, Exalted One, for the blessings you've bestowed upon my family."

She almost imagined she heard, "You're welcome, child."

Smiling, she drifted to sleep.

9

ONE MONTH LATER

Summer grabbed Autumn's wrist and dragged her into the closest room, putting her finger to her lips until she shut the door.

"I can't find it!"

"It?"

"Yes, it. *It!* Coop's wedding ring." A full meltdown was imminent.

"What did you do with it?"

Giving her sister the universal look for *you've got to be fucking kidding me*, Summer threw up her hands. "If I knew that, I wouldn't be here, freaking out on *you*! I'd be getting ready to walk down the aisle." She picked up the tulle hem of her dress and started to pace. "I can't get married without that ring. Coop and I spent two hours designing our matching set, and Knox went through the trouble to make them for us." Stopping, she fanned her face, overly warm in her heightened state of panic. "I'm drawing a blank, and even if I could remember the design, I can't just conjure another one, Tums. I'm a water elemental, not metal. *What am I going to do?*"

The meltdown was no longer imminent. It was upon her.

With a small shake of her head, her sister sashayed forward, her hands resting firmly on her hips. "It's simple. Have Knox make you a new one."

"You don't understand. He mined the metal or some shi—"

"*Don't swear!* We don't need the entire rodent population of Leiper's Fork showing up on our doorstep."

"Pregnant, remember? No mice will show while I'm carrying another Thorne." Summer buried her face in her hands. "And Coop will understand, won't he?" Shaking her head, she groaned. "I can already picture his disappointment."

"Trust me, sister. It's going to be all right."

"You don't know that. How does it look, starting off a marriage without a ring to give to your new husband? *The* ring. The one lovingly designed together. Explaining that I was so irresponsible as to lose it in less than a month's time?"

"It's Coop, and he loves you, Summer. You're being a Bridezilla."

"How can you even say that right now? I'm so far removed from a Bridezilla!"

Amusement flashed in her sister's amber eyes, and a smirk curled one side of her mouth. "Really? Next, you're going to tell me that you didn't have Spring change the color of the lilies five different times or that you didn't have Winnie, who was trying to bake you the perfect wedding cake, alter the frosting from vanilla, to lemon, to chocolate, back to lemon, all within a two-hour span?"

Too stunned for words, Summer stared. *Had* she done that? The planning had been a blur. Which was probably why she couldn't remember where she'd put the blasted ring in the first place.

"It's okay." Autumn wrapped her in a tight hug. "Really. None of us have minded, and dress shopping was fun for Mama and me."

That last bit sounded extremely tongue in cheek.

"But GiGi conjured a... *Oh.* I was a bear about the dress, too, wasn't I?"

Her sister held her index finger and thumb an inch apart but remained quiet. Which, for her snarky sibling, was a feat.

"None of it matters without the ring." Summer absently glanced at her familiar, who suddenly appeared too innocent by far, and frowned. "Saul?"

"What?" He put a paw to his chest, puffed up his tail, and looked around with fake indignation. Or maybe it wasn't fake. One could never tell with her squirrel. "You blamin' me? Me? Like I'd take your freakin' ring?"

The longer he protested, the more Summer was convinced he knew *something*. She squinted her eyes in a threatening manner. "Saul."

"I don't freaking know nothin'."

"Saauuul."

"What? I'm not a rat fink!"

Autumn picked him up by the scruff of his neck. "Spill it, furball. Where's the ring?"

"Saul, *please*." Summer rescued him from her sister, not convinced Autumn wouldn't fry his fuzzy butt to get the info she needed. Sure, Summer wanted answers, but the tiny thug was connected to her on a cosmic level and still one of the Goddess's creatures. "Please tell me where it is. I can't get married without it."

"Good riddance, I say. Coop's a mudderfuc—"

"*Saul!*" Summer and Autumn hollered in unison.

"You promised to be nice!" Summer said, reminding him of their conversation the previous month.

But her familiar had worked up a full head of steam, and there was no stopping his rant. "He said I had a screw loose! *Can you believe that?*" His pint-sized body was vibrating in the palm of her hand. "Me! A screw loose!"

Autumn opened her mouth to speak, but Summer frantically shook her head, praying to the Goddess that Saul didn't turn around and see the retort forming on her sister's lips.

"I should've shanked him when I had the chance. Never did believe he was good enough for you. And neither did Rocco or any of the others."

"I love him, Saul. He puts both Olivia's and my needs above all others." She ran a calming hand down her familiar's back and smiled as his anger melted away under her touch. "You have to admit, Coop has come a long way from when we first got together."

Autumn snorted.

"You don't think so?" A sick feeling settled in the pit of Summer's stomach. There had been a lot of misunderstandings and breakups back then. Too many for her liking. And now, the others acted as if they knew something she didn't, and she was going to feel foolish if she learned anything bad about Coop at this stage.

"Oh, no, I *do*. One thousand percent. I just think it's funny you're trying to reason with the squirrel mafia's kingpin, one who has a brain the size of a pea, I might add."

"Pea?! Why, I'll..." In the face of Autumn's challenging stare, Saul backed down, but not without grumbling under his breath.

"We're losing the point of the conversation here.

Where's the ring?" Summer demanded, done with the games.

"Can't say."

"Can't or won't?"

"Can't. I've been spelled to secrecy."

"Oh, for fuck's sake!" Autumn scooped him from Summer's palm. "You stay here, sister, and I'll get to the bottom of this." With that, she sailed out the door, leaving Summer to recommence her meltdown.

"WE'VE GOT A PROBLEM, C.C."

Coop turned from where he was straightening his tie in the cheval mirror and glared at Keaton. "I fucking hate those words. Every single time you say them, it's more than a problem. It's a crisis." He dropped his head back and inhaled deeply. When he was marginally more centered, he asked, "What's the problem?"

"I can't find the ring."

His stomach dropped. "Which ring?" But he suspected he already knew.

"*Your* ring. Or rather, the ring you intended to give to Summer." Keaton looked ill.

Coop gripped his brother's upper arms and gave him a hard shake. "What do you mean? Where the hell did it go?"

"I don't know. One second, it was in the box on the dresser in Zane's room, then it was gone."

"Jesus H! You had *one* job, Keat. *One!* And I can't get married without it. Summer and I designed those damned rings. Where am I supposed to come up with one in"—he checked his watch—"less than an hour? I'm a fire elemental and a piss-poor one at that. It's not like *I* can remake it."

"Didn't Knox create them in the first place? Get him to whip up another one."

"He mined the metal. From some sacred place that can only be accessed at the peak of the lunar cycle or some mystical crap like that." Coop ran shaking fingers through his hair. "Summer's going to be heartbroken."

And in turn, he would, too. He'd bruised her heart on one-too-many occasions in the past, mostly with doubts and misunderstandings. Oh, she'd put on a brave face because that's what Summer did when faced with adversity, but Coop never wanted to see disappointment in her wide blue eyes again. His stomach churned at the thought.

"We'll find it, C.C."

"Let's start where you saw it last. Maybe the dresser got bumped, and it rolled under…"

The emphatic shaking of Keaton's head made him want to wallop his brother. *What best man loses the ring?*

"I've already checked."

"We are damned well going to check again. As a

matter of fact, we're going to look under every piece of furniture in that freaking room, and then we're going to look in the vacuum cleaner canister just in case one of the Thornes went crazy cleaning this morning."

"Dude, they're a family of witches. They don't clean when they can snap their fingers and have everything pristine in a second."

Coop shoved his brother, none too gently, toward the door. "Come on."

As soon as he whipped open the door, Coop saw Autumn hurrying down the hall. The second she spotted them, she stopped short and tucked one arm behind her back. An uncomfortable expression flashed across her face, quickly replaced by her standard sassy smile.

"Hey, fellas. What's up?"

"I lost—"

Coop clamped his hand over Keaton's big mouth and cast Autumn a tight smile. "His socks. He lost his lucky socks. And he refuses to finish dressing until we find them."

Autumn's eyes flared wide like she was positive it wasn't socks but their damned minds that went missing. And she wouldn't be wrong if that was at all what she suspected.

After a quick glance toward Keaton's feet, she frowned and nodded. "Yeah, okay."

A muffled squeak sounded from behind her, and

her expression shifted toward guilty before she masked it.

"What was that?" Coop demanded.

"What?"

"That squeak."

"What squeak?"

"Autumn," he growled.

She gave him a sickly grin. "Oh! *That* squeak. Just Saul. Gotta run!"

With a simple snap of her fingers, she was gone, leaving Coop with his hand still clamped over Keaton's downturned mouth.

His brother shoved Coop away and glared. "You've lost your damned mind, C.C."

"Yeah, I'm afraid that's what your wife thinks, too. And I will if we don't find that ring. Come on."

Halfway to their destination, he stopped and turned back toward the spot where Autumn had disappeared. "Don't you think the thing with Saul was weird?"

"Everything with Saul is weird. Why should today be any different?" Keaton tried to keep walking, but Coop gripped his arm and stopped him.

"I'm serious, Keaton. Why would Autumn have Saul with her when he's Summer's familiar? He's never far from her unless he's forced to be."

"How should I know? C.C., we have to find the ring. We don't have time to worry about why my wife might be babysitting that crazy-ass squirrel."

"I feel it in my bones, man. Something's up with those two."

His brother sighed heavily. "Go find her, then. I'll look in Zane's room again."

Ignoring his instincts and giving up the mystery, Coop shook his head. "No. I'll go with you to look. We don't have any time to spare."

10

"*He* won't say."

Summer stopped pacing to acknowledge Autumn's return. "Where did he scurry off to?"

"I locked him in the pantry to consider the error of his ways." Her sister huffed on her nails and buffed them on the bodice of her tangerine bridesmaid dress. "It shouldn't take him long for his memory to be restored. I told him I'd hog-tie him to Eddie's trunk if he didn't start remembering soon."

"Tums! You can't—"

Autumn waved her hand in dismissal and plopped down on the closest chair. "Oh, stop. It's not like I intended to leave him locked away. I gave Winnie instructions to release him in five minutes if I'm not back."

"But we're still no closer to finding the ring." Summer moaned and flung herself back on the bed.

"Are you sure you brought it from the house? In all the chaos, you may have left it on your dresser at home."

"No. I had it here, for sure." She frowned as she thought back to when she arrived that morning. "Or I think I did. Anyway, Saul knows something. I'm positive of it. We just need to get him talking." With a grim determination, Summer stood and began the painstaking process of removing her clothes.

"What are you doing?" Autumn jumped up to stay her hands. "You don't have time to get out of and back into this monstrosity."

Gasping, Summer spun around and glared. "You said it was a beautiful dress! Were you really going to let me walk down the aisle in something that was awful?"

"Oh, for the love of the Goddess!" Her sister sandwiched Summer's face between her palms. "Breathe. And think. Even if I were inclined to pull a prank of that nature, Aunt GiGi and Mama wouldn't. Your dress is gorgeous. As are you. I just meant that it's a chore to put on and take off manually, and you refuse to use magic to do it, for some godforsaken reason."

"I'm emotionally charged today, Tums. What if I lose control of my power and destroy the dress?" Tears shimmered in Summer's eyes, making her sister one big blur. "I'm a freaking mess."

"Yes, you are, but so is every woman on her wedding day. Since I'm not emotionally charged, is it okay if I help you the old-fashioned Thorne way?"

Summer nodded and turned to give her sister access to the billions of bow ties holding her filmy dress together. Within seconds, they were all undone and the dress was sagging open.

After laying it on the bed, she drew on her robe and cinched it tight. "Okay. Let's do this thing. Where do we look first?"

"Where would Saul hide a box that size? Does he have any special places he likes to store things?"

Smacking her forehead with the heel of her hand, Summer blew out a breath. "Of course! Why didn't I think of that?" With a shake of her head, she charged for the door. "I know exactly where he would stash it. Let's go."

"Wait! It's bad luck for Coop to see the bride on your wedding day."

"That's *in* the dress, Tums. I'm wearing a waffle robe, and I'm pretty sure there are no superstitions attached to that."

"Right, okay." Still, Autumn eased the door open and peered both ways before grabbing Summer's hand and dragging her toward the stairs.

Just as they got to the landing, one of the doors opened on the floor below them.

"Cloak us!" Summer hissed, panicked in case

Autumn was right about the bad luck seeing a bride in any state of dress or lack thereof.

Her sister whispered the words to effectively conceal them at the exact moment Coop and Keaton came into view. Looking haggard with his hair a tousled mess, Coop charged toward the stairs—and right at them!

With a small yelp of surprise, Summer latched onto Autumn and bolted up the steps. They pressed themselves flat against the wall of closets as the brothers passed by.

"This is hopeless, C.C.," Keaton lamented.

"Shut it and keep searching. That damned thing has to be here somewhere."

"But—"

"Keaton, I need you to stop with the Negative Nelly routine and help me. Or better yet, find your wife and discover what she was doing with Saul." Coop stopped short and turned in the direction of the linen closets. With a frown, he gestured their way. "You don't think that demented squirrel is taking his revenge on me, do you? Like maybe he hid it where we wouldn't think to look?"

For a heart-stopping moment, Summer thought maybe he was talking to her, but it was Keaton who answered.

"Well, you did say he had a screw loose," Keaton said dryly.

"Because he does!" Coop retorted. "He threatened

to castrate me. *In front of witnesses.* Saul has lost his last marble, if he had any to begin with."

Part of Summer wanted to defend her familiar, but she wasn't feeling particularly charitable toward him at the moment, so she let Coop's insult stand. Besides, he hadn't figured out she and Autumn were standing only a few feet away, and Summer didn't intend to reveal herself.

"What do you think they're looking for?" Autumn's eyes were narrowed on her husband. "Doesn't it sound like they are having a similar problem to ours?"

"If Saul is trying to sabotage my wedding to Coop, I'll shave him bald!" Summer ground out. "Let's go get him."

"Don't you think we should follow Frick and Frack?" Autumn gestured with her thumb to the retreating men.

"Nah. Once we grab my tiny troublemaker, we'll scry to see what Coop and Keaton are up to."

Ten minutes later, Summer never wanted to strangle her familiar more.

"WE DON'T HAVE much time. Any minute now, they'll notice their rings are missing." Alastair looked at the new inscription on Summer's wedding ring and smiled. "You do great work, my friend."

Damian Dethridge, also known as the Aether in the

magical community, grunted and sent Alastair a dark look. "Of course I do, Al. I'm the bloody Aether. Do you want the same inscription on this one, or do you want to change the spell up for Cooper's ring?"

"You don't have a spell to make him stop questioning my authority in that book of yours, do you? No? Fine, use the same one as you did for Summer's."

With a laugh, Damian went to work, blessing the second ring.

The enchantment placed on the jewelry was meant to protect both Summer and Coop and, by extension, their home and family. When his beloved Olivia was born last year, Alastair had Damian perform a ceremony to safeguard her, just as he had Summer and Holly when they were small children. If he could go back in time, he'd have had Preston do the same for his three daughters so they would never have experienced the hardships they'd endured at the hands of Alastair's greatest enemy. But he wasn't a Traveler, and in the end, the Thorne women had come out stronger for their experiences.

As Alastair watched Damian finish the spell for the ring, the new inscription with an infinity symbol on either side appeared with a flare of yellow-white light.

Two hearts, one enduring love.

"Do you think they'll appreciate the quote?"

Alastair glanced up from admiring Damian's handiwork. "Summer will. Who knows about Coop? He might be irritated he didn't think of it first." He held his hand out for the second ring. "I have to sneak these back into their rooms via that nutty squirrel Summer calls a familiar."

"Why not just be upfront and give them back to them at the ceremony?"

With a grin and a slap on his friend's back, he asked, "Where's the fun in that?"

Five minutes later, Alastair was confronted by Rorie. "Summer's missing!"

"What do you mean she's missing? She was in her room, getting ready, when I left."

"But she's nowhere to be found, and Autumn has disappeared with her."

After a tired sigh, he tugged down his cuffs and glanced around the foyer, summing up the scene. Winnie, Spring, and Holly all wore concerned expressions similar to their mother's. "When was the last time anyone saw the two of them?"

"I did." Winnie frowned and nodded toward the kitchen. "About the time Autumn decided to lock Saul in the pantry. She told me to let him out in five minutes if she wasn't back for him."

"But she gave no indication where she was going?"
"None."

"Did any of you think to scry?" he asked patiently.

Rorie smacked his arm. "I'm offended you had to ask, darling. Of course we did."

Turning abruptly, he left them alone in the hallway

and strode to the kitchen. He called back to Winnie. "Where's Saul now, child?"

"Missing from the cabinet. The door was open when I went back for him."

"Lovely," he muttered.

Once he reached the sink, he lifted a glass from the drainer and filled it with water.

"Ostendo!"

The water became cloudy and swirled in a clockwise direction, reminiscent of a tornado, wider at the top and narrowing at the bottom of the glass. When the liquid became clear again, he could see Summer arguing with Saul as Autumn looked ready to pop his overblown head off his tiny shoulders.

"They're fine. Simply cloaked with Granny Thorne's spell." He dumped the water down the sink and placed the glass upside down in the drainer, then faced the women behind him. "They're in the old elephant barn, arguing with Saul. A useless endeavor on both their parts."

"Bloody hell!" Rorie scowled at Winnie. "I thought you said Zane looked there."

"He did! But apparently, they didn't want to make themselves known to him."

"Fine. I'll go myself." She glared at Alastair and poked his chest hard enough to make him wince. "When I get back, you'll bloody well tell me where you hied off to and why. In the meantime, make yourself useful and get everyone to their seats on the front lawn."

As his mate stormed away, Alastair grinned his appreciation for her feistiness. He wasn't fast enough to sober when she spun back around.

"If this is another of your games, Alastair Thorne, we'll have a serious discussion after the ceremony." She gave him a stern look, then pointed skyward. "You and Winnie mind the weather. I want nothing but sunshine today."

He snapped to attention and saluted. "Yes, ma'am."

"I've got your ma'am right here." With a shake of her fist, she sailed out the door.

"Goddess, I love that woman."

A commotion on the stairs drew them out into the foyer. Coop and Keaton stopped mid-step when they saw him. The wave of nervousness from the men struck Alastair at the same time their eyes widened in alarm.

"Why so harried, gentlemen?" Alastair asked smoothly as he approached the two.

Keaton opened his mouth but got an elbow to the ribs for his troubles.

"Harried? I'm not harried." Coop looked at his brother. "Are you harried? See, sir, no one is harried."

Alastair bit back a grin. "Hmm. Then you must be on your way to the altar. Let me escort you."

Face pale, Coop appeared ready to swallow his tongue.

"We can't!" Keaton blurted.

"We can't?" It took a second for Coop to catch on. "Oh! That's right. We can't. Tell him why we can't, Keat."

"Really, dude? I'm trying to save your bacon, and you throw me under the bus? You couldn't come up with an excuse?"

Shoving down a laugh, Alastair raised his brows and stared down his nose at the brothers. "It's a wonder your parents didn't lose their sanity with the two of you." With a fake put-upon sigh, he said, "I believe it's time for you to tell us what's going on."

11

"*I* swear to the Goddess, Saul! If you don't tell me where that ring is right now—"

Autumn gripped Summer's arm and pointed toward the entrance of the elephant barn. "Mama just walked in, and she's not looking too thrilled at the moment."

"Drop the cloak, my dears. The gig is up," Rorie said, glaring at what, to her, would be an empty aisle. "I'll give you to the count of—ah! There you are. Would you mind explaining what the bloody hell is going on? Why aren't you in your dress, Summer? Have you changed your mind?"

"No!" Summer held Saul up over her head like a trophy and gave him a little shake. In his nervousness, he released a single oval dropping that fell at her feet. "Ew. Not cool, Saul." To her mother, she said, "I can't find Coop's ring, and I'm positive Saul has something to do with it."

A startled expression crossed her mother's face before she quickly concealed it and narrowed her eyes. "Your father has a lot of explaining to do."

"Dad? Why..."

The instant she mentioned her father, Saul's stubborn resistance melted, and he started singing like a caged canary. "It was your freaking father's fault. I didn't want to do it, but he—"

"That's enough, Saul," Alastair boomed from behind them. "Summer, release your familiar, preferably in the wild where he'll get lost, and meet me in your room. I believe you'll find what you're looking for."

"Coop's wedding ring?" She was afraid to hope, unsure why her father would play such a dirty trick, today of all days.

"Coop's ring," he said with a soft smile. "You won't believe this, but I was actually trying to do something thoughtful."

"By stealing the one thing I needed to get married?" The volume and shrill tone of her voice caused everyone around her to wince, but she was past caring. Her day was almost ruined by whatever wacky plan her father had enacted.

"I didn't steal it, child. I borrowed it." His warm, caring expression made her want to hit him. Or cry.

Probably cry because he was being kind. "For Damian to bless," Alastair added.

"Oh, Dad." She sniffed and used the sleeve of her waffle robe to dab at her eyes. "Why didn't you just say so?"

"I wanted it to be a surprise when you and Cooper saw your rings for the first time."

"Wait! What?" Autumn pushed in front of Summer to glare at Alastair. "Are you telling me you stole"—she waved a hand in dismissal when he would've protested —"*borrowed* the other ring from Coop, too?"

Without waiting for him to respond, she turned to Summer. "I *knew* they were up to something!"

"They?" Alastair asked dryly. So dryly, in fact, Summer had a darned good idea he knew exactly who *they* were.

"Coop and Keaton were running around the house like chickens with their heads cut off," Autumn replied. "They had to be looking for the lost ring."

Seized by a mischief demon, Summer smiled evilly. "You don't by chance still have it, do you, Dad? I mean, knowing you, you left them to sweat it out."

"I do, indeed. Why?"

"I think you should wait to give it to him until the ceremony. Let him freak out a little longer."

Alastair's dark-blond brows shot to his hairline. "You want to start your marriage by torturing your husband?"

"Yes."

"Since it's for a good cause, mum's the word."

She didn't miss the delighted twinkle in his eye or the play of a smile on his lips. Alastair was the king of keeping secrets, and he never revealed she was behind letting Coop sweat for a bit longer than necessary.

Summer looked at Autumn. "Do you know your role?"

"To make Keaton just as miserably guilty as Coop? Abso-freaking-lutely. I live for this shit."

"Then let's go torture those Carlyle boys. Just like old times."

Alastair put his arm around Rorie. "I've never been prouder of my family than at this moment."

"I swear, Alastair Thorne, if you aren't causing trouble, you're not happy," she said with an affectionate smile.

Summer snorted a laugh, happy to see her parents together and still so in love after all these years. That's what she wanted for Coop and her. The unconditional love, the humor, the solidarity, the passion, the friendship. Those were the five things that made a true marriage.

Meeting her father's considering gaze, she winked. And when he grinned, Summer felt her whole world was right.

"Where's Olivia?"

"Coop's parents are with her, Chloe, and Jolyon," he said as he glanced down at his watch. "You have precisely five minutes to get changed and downstairs. Do you need your mother's help?"

"I think I've got this." And surprisingly, Summer felt like she did. Her fear of accidentally destroying her dress with magic had passed, and she would welcome the five minutes alone to center herself. "Will you hold on to the ring I intend to give Coop, Dad? Give them to both of us at the same time?"

"So you can pretend you knew I had them all along?"

"Exactly."

COOP COULDN'T BELIEVE his terrible luck. He and Keaton had turned the house upside down to no avail. The symbol of his enduring love for Summer was gone, and he only had himself to blame for letting the ring out of his sight to begin with.

As he descended the stairs to the foyer for the final time before his wedding, he had the sensation of walking to the gallows—but in reverse. One usually ascended steps to a hanging. He shook his head to rid himself of his morose thoughts and tried to recapture the excitement he'd felt earlier in the day, before Summer's ring went missing.

Alastair greeted him in the foyer, and the sparkle in the other man's eyes caused all kinds of suspicions to gather in Coop's mind.

Surely, a father wouldn't try to sabotage his own daughter's wedding.

It's not like Alastair held any love for him, but as far as Coop knew, the guy didn't *hate* him.

But maybe he did.

Alastair cocked his blond head to study him a moment, and Coop understood this was the man's way of summing up a situation and all the feelings of those associated with it. His empath ability allowed Alastair to read the room like no other.

"You're in turmoil, son. Unless you intend to jilt my daughter, there's no need to be," Alastair assured him.

"I lost Summer's wedding ring," Coop blurted. His eyes widened in horror at his diarrhea of the mouth. Why in the Goddess's name he had regurgitated that information was anyone's guess. Perhaps, like some of the criminals he'd put away, he needed to confess to assuage his guilt.

Other than for Alastair's brows to shoot up, his reaction was tame.

Too tame.

Coop narrowed his eyes. "What do you know about the ring, old man?"

"*Old man?* Do you have a death wish, Cooper?"

Normally, he'd have said no, but maybe the part of him that didn't want to disappoint Summer would rather be struck down by Alastair than face her with the truth.

"Maybe a small one," Coop finally said with a wry

smile. Overhead, the sound of Summer's laughter could be heard above that of the women and girls with her. He glanced up at the ceiling and smiled involuntarily at the joyful quality of her laugh.

"Thank you for recognizing how special my daughter truly is."

Shocked by Alastair's sudden sentiment, Coop could only stare.

"Close your mouth, my boy. You'll catch flies."

With a small shake of his head and a chuckle, Coop shook Alastair's hand. "I'm just grateful she's stubborn and refused to give up on me when she could've and probably should've."

"Some people take a little longer to accept change. You had a lot thrust on you in a short amount of time. She understands that." Alastair's grip tightened over his. "But now that you've acclimated to the witch world, you've no reason to ever break her heart again. Correct?"

Oddly, the show of force didn't intimidate Coop like it probably should've. Maybe it was because he had no intention of ever hurting Summer and felt confident of that fact. "Mr. Thorne, I love your daughter with every fiber of my being, and I'll spend every day of my life reminding her that I do."

"Good enough. Make your way to the altar. You'll find your brother outside, waiting for you."

Coop was halfway to the door when an idea occurred to him. "Do you think you could conjure a temporary ring for me to give her? Just until I can find the missing one. So she's not embarrassed during the ceremony." He almost stuttered over the request, feeling like a careless fool for having to ask in the first place.

"Something can be arranged. I'll have a ring for you by the time you're ready to exchange your vows."

Coop had never experienced a more heartfelt gratitude, with the exception of when Summer gave him a second chance after he'd royally screwed up their courtship. Perhaps Summer didn't need to be disappointed at all.

He returned to Alastair's side and used his smartphone to show him a picture of the original design. "If you can make it look like this, I can wait until after the ceremony to tell her I lost the one Knox created."

"Of course." Alastair barely spared the image a glance, and he checked his watch impatiently. "Anything else?"

"No. Thank you, sir."

With a slight smile, Alastair nodded and turned away, leaving Coop to believe he might just hang him out to dry. But surely, he wouldn't ruin his own daughter's wedding in such a way, right?

Coop made a pit stop to the downstairs powder room. As a fire elemental, he ran hot, and the added stress of this particular situation had completely engulfed him, causing him to become excessively warm. He needed to find a way to cool down, or he'd combust. Taking a spare moment, he stripped down to the waist, and using the hand towel, he wet it and wiped down his entire torso, rung it out, and repeated. Then he held the damp towel to the back of his neck to cool his body temperature. When he finally felt marginally less overheated, he dressed, straightened his tie, fussed with his hair, and smoothed his tux.

It was go time.

If Summer didn't leave him at the altar, he'd be a married man within twenty minutes. With a smile for his reflection, he nodded, intent on making this wedding the best experience possible for her. His love for her required it. He opened the door and stepped into the hall full of hope and determination.

---

12

*A*s Summer stood within the walls of the temporary tent by the side of the house, she closed her eyes and inhaled slowly to the count of four, then exhaled for the same count. She did this five more times, striving for tranquility and to prepare for her upcoming vows.

During the planning stages, she'd explained to Coop how this type of ceremony worked. How their souls would connect on a deeper level after today due to the handfasting ritual. Damian Dethridge, with the permission of the Goddess Isis, would bind their souls together and bless them in the process. They would become two halves of the same whole.

Coop had stated he understood, but Summer couldn't help but have misgivings. Yes, in the time they'd been in a relationship, he'd mellowed somewhat. The rigid, unrelenting side of him had learned a few tough lessons when it came to magic and the Thornes. Family was everything to them, and while Coop was a welcome addition, Summer and her immediate family had an unbreakable bond. They would always drop everything to be there for each other—without fail. Regardless of which side of the law their escapades fell on. And now, he would be marrying into that world, and it could possibly test his sense of right and wrong if things went sideways and unknown enemies rose up to, once again, disrupt their lives.

"Are you okay, sister?"

Summer opened her eyes and met Autumn's concerned gaze. "I think so."

Winnie approached and wrapped an arm around her. "What's the problem?"

How could Summer explain her reaction was a post-traumatic response to when Coop was on and off again in those days before they moved to North Carolina? That her nerves were whacked-out from the ring debacle and her memories were returning to taunt her with the what-ifs of him deciding she was too much? That her family was too much?

"I recognize that look." Holly shooed their sisters away and approached. Placing her hands on either side of Summer's face, she gazed deeply into her eyes. "You're on the verge of a panic attack, Summer. For a while, I suffered through those after Quentin and

Frankie changed our timeline." With light fingers, she massaged Summer's temples. "You have to breathe and remember everything is going to be just fine. Coop's out there, anxiously waiting for you to join him, and if he had cold feet, you'd have known it long before today."

"He still doesn't love magic and prefers normal most days. That's not us." Summer gestured to all of them and gnawed her lip. "What if it gets to be too much for him again?"

"It won't." A sparkle lit Holly's jade eyes. "Can I confess something?"

Summer nodded jerkily.

"Every single time Quentin returns from a traveling mission, I have him tell me what he knows of our family's future."

"And Coop and I are happy together?"

"Yep. You and Coop have a forever kind of love, sis. And that isn't going away in any alternate reality."

Tears of relief flooded Summer's eyes, blurring Holly's beloved face. "Thank you, Hol."

"You deserve to be happy, and you will be." She handed Summer a tissue. "Today is a celebration of your love. It's meant to be a joyous occasion, and it will be once your nerves settle and you realize I'm right."

"Coop loves you, sister," Autumn added. "Anyone can tell by watching the two of you together."

Summer smiled, albeit a little sadly. "I know he

does. That was never in question. I'm just freaking out about long-term and how much he's willing to put up with."

"You'll get your assurance after he commits today, but I really don't think he's ever going anywhere," Winnie said with a sweet smile. "Zane told me that Coop has mentioned countless times how blessed he is. You and Olivia are all he can talk about."

"Olivia!" Summer put her palm to her forehead. "I forgot to check—"

Autumn soothed her with a hand on her arm. "She's fine and being cared for. Don't worry about Ollie."

Sabrina, who had been waiting at the tent opening with Chloe, approached with a purpose. "I can show you the future, Miss Summer. Papa doesn't like it when I do, but if it will make you feel better, I can show you."

The Aether's daughter was known to blurt out predictions when trouble was about to descend on someone she liked, regardless of her father's rule to keep such things to herself. Looking into the obsidian eyes of the girl, Summer could see the clarity and calm Sabrina possessed. There was no troubled expression or worry lurking anywhere to be seen. And for that reason, she rejected the kind offer.

"Thank you, Sabrina. I have the feeling if this was a bad idea, you'd have already said so." The sunny smile

Summer received bolstered her resolve and dissolved the last of her fears. "I think you gave me the gift of security without breaking your word to your father, didn't you?"

"Maybe. Can I change the flowers to purple, Miss Summer? I think they would be prettier," Sabrina said with a sly grin.

"You are a master negotiator, kid. It's a good thing purple is one of my absolute favorite colors." Summer smiled as she tapped Sabrina's nose. "Should we change the bridesmaid dresses, too?"

Eyes wide with hero worship, Sabrina nodded.

"You and Chloe can go to town and have fun with it."

The girls squealed and lit their tent with brilliant bolts of color as they tried to find the perfect shade of purple to suit their tastes. Summer laughed along with her sisters as Sabrina and Chloe chattered happily. Their joy went a long way to ease her stress.

Alastair peeked his head through the tent opening. "It's time, my dear. Preston's waiting outside."

"He can come in, Dad." She looked at Autumn. "Ready to herd the girls for the long walk down the aisle?"

"I'm on it."

Preston and Alastair held back the sides of the tent so the wedding procession could line up. Chloe and Sabrina were dressed in matching amethyst dresses with a fluorescent green bow around the waist. They carried pale-yellow baskets full of the rainbow-colored flowers they'd decided on.

Other than to lift a brow and shoot Summer an amused glance, Alastair said nothing about their bizarre color palette. One by one, her sisters lined up from youngest to oldest, each with a new deep-purple dress and bright green shoes.

"Wasn't Autumn wearing a tangerine-colored gown earlier?" Alastair asked as he held out an arm for Summer to take.

"She was. Sabrina and Chloe decided purple was a far better color for my wedding."

Preston laughed. "Will it match what the men are wearing?"

Summer shrugged. "I'm not all that worried about clashing with the guys. But those chartreuse shoes are an eyesore," she said dryly.

Both men laughed heartily, causing her to giggle. No longer at odds over the events of the past, the brothers shared a smile.

"Are you ready to give our daughter away, brother?" Preston asked Alastair.

"If you are."

"I don't know if I'll ever be ready." Voice choked with emotion, Preston gazed down at her, his honey-amber eyes shining with love. "You're beautiful, my sunshine. I don't know if a lovelier bride ever existed."

Summer flung herself into his strong arms and closed her eyes as he embraced her. All the times she'd run to him as a little girl, expecting and receiving his help to heal a hurt, came flooding back. "Thank you, Daddy. And thank you for always being there for me."

"You may not be mine by blood, but you'll always be my beloved daughter." He cleared his throat and gave her a soft smile. "I'm just glad I could be here for your big day."

"Me, too."

Alastair held out a handkerchief to her, and Summer accepted it with a grateful look. She hadn't realized she was crying until that moment.

"Thanks, Dad," she managed to say past a thick throat packed with emotion.

"You're welcome, child." He glanced between Preston and her. "Should I step back and allow Preston today's honor?"

"No." Preston gripped Alastair's shoulder and squeezed. "We'll do this together. You've earned your place in her life."

"I love you both so much," she cried.

Her father kissed her forehead, then stepped back and tugged on his cuffs. "Dry your tears, my dear. This is supposed to be a happy day. Although, I can see where it might be a little overwhelming. After all, you're marrying that thick-headed Carlyle boy."

That made her laugh, as she realized it was supposed to. "Are you ever going to cut him a break?"

"Where's the fun in that?"

SUMMER STEPPED AROUND THE CORNER, and Coop exhaled his relief the moment he saw her. She was breathtaking in a flowing white confection, hair mostly pinned up, with the rest spilling over one breast. Feet bare and one hand on the arm of each of the Thorne brothers, she looked like a goddess being escorted by her consorts, and Coop was never more awestruck.

Alastair and Preston wore matching tuxedoes, and they looked like movie stars from a bygone era. But they were a formidable duo, those men. Not for the first time, Coop felt intimidated and unworthy of joining their family.

As if sensing his troubled thoughts, Alastair caught and held his gaze. There was a slight inclination of his head and a wink, and oddly, the gesture took away any remaining anxiety Coop felt about marrying Summer. *She* had never been the issue. Her drama-packed life was another matter. But today, no enemies were coming out of the woodwork, and other than the ring fiasco, there were no problems lingering in the background, ready to destroy a life.

When Summer's luminescent blue eyes met his across the distance, Coop silently thanked his lucky stars that she'd fallen in love with him all those years before and that she was tenacious. If not, he'd have screwed up beyond repair and he'd never know the healing power of true love or the joys it could bring.

Beside him, Keaton stood tall and silent. As Summer and her fathers approached, Coop's brother bumped him and leaned in to say, "Don't fuck this up."

It was enough to relieve the tension building in Coop's chest, and he laughed. "I don't intend to."

"Good. She and Olivia are the best things to ever happen to you."

"I know." Stepping forward, Coop met the trio, and once Summer tucked her arm through his, he first shook Preston's hand, then Alastair's. "Thank you for the precious gift you are entrusting to me, gentlemen. I've never been more honored."

Preston gave him an approving nod, and Alastair grinned. "Nicely said, son."

"Take care of our daughter," Preston added with a formidable stare. It brought to mind the first meeting in the man's study when he'd judged Coop's worth and found him lacking. At the time, Preston Thorne hadn't been wrong.

"Always, sir." Coop looked down into Summer's trusting eyes. There was no nervousness in her expression. No worry. Just love, and Coop was humbled by her continued faith in him. He lifted her hand and brought it to his lips. "Always," he promised her, then kissed her knuckles.

Together, they walked up the steps to the temporary platform created for the wedding. The corner poles were decorated with a wide arrangement of flowers and vines, all real and conjured by Spring Thorne. Massive, forty-eight-inch-wide bows secured the sheer swag of material that ran from one column to the next, adding to the romantic setting.

In the center of the platform, Summer's sisters, acting as bridesmaids, were lined up to the left, and Coop's groomsmen were on the right. About ten minutes earlier, their cummerbunds had mysteriously changed from soft orange to a deep purple that matched the dresses of Summer's attendants. No one bothered to question why. It was the side effect of living with a whimsical witch.

In the divide between the two groups stood the Aether, Damian Dethridge, the most magically super-charged human being on the planet and one scary mo-fo. Hundreds of years old, he looked to be about thirty-seven. His eyes were so dark as to be black, matching his hair and his sleek suit. Damian looked like Coop imagined the Devil himself would. Mysterious, formidable, and ungodly handsome. So gorgeous, in fact, he made the men around him exceedingly uncomfortable whenever he was present. But Damian's arrogance wasn't lent to his appearance. In fact, Coop would say the man wasn't arrogant at all, merely sure of himself and his abilities.

"Are you ready to exchange your vows?" Damian asked. His voice, smooth as silk and hypnotic to a degree, was still loud enough to be heard by the congregation.

Coop looked down at Summer to find her staring back at him.

"We are," they said in unison.

"Excellent. Let's get started."

13

I bet you thought I'd forgotten this part, didn't you? Nope! Still skipping this chapter as per tradition. ;)

14

*D*amian held a metal bowl and a long white cloth shot through with silver threads—the handfasting material handed down through the Thorne family line from Isis.

"Are you ready, Summer?" he asked with a soft smile.

She nodded. "I am."

Damian faced Coop. "Are you ready, Cooper?"

"I am," Coop confirmed with a nod.

"Then let us proceed. Who has the rings?" the Aether asked.

Coop looked at Keaton, but his brother shrugged and shook his head. With a wild look at Autumn to see if perhaps she had them, Coop opened his mouth to profess his guilt and beg Summer's forgiveness.

"That would be me." Alastair climbed the steps and

opened his fisted hand. Sitting in his palm were two rings, one sized for Summer's hand and one for Coop's. They looked identical to the two Knox had originally designed.

A wave of suspicion crashed over Coop, and he scowled at Alastair. "You had them all along?"

"Actually, we both did," Damian said with an amused half smile. "Alastair wanted to have them blessed and a protection spell added with an inscription."

All the horrible things Coop had ever thought about Alastair's deception faded away as he accepted the jewelry. "So no replica needed," he murmured with a shake of his head.

"No, son," Alastair replied just as low. "No replica needed. I took them while the two of you were dressing, hoping to replace them before you noticed they were gone. I wasn't quick enough."

Summer bit her lip, and her eyes twinkled with the laughter she was barely holding back.

"Why do I have the feeling you knew and were letting me sweat it?" Coop narrowed his eyes.

"Well, initially, I was sweating it just as much, if not more, than you were. Dad showed up just as we were ready to murder Saul."

"Too bad he wasn't a few minutes later," Coop quipped.

Summer's eyes went wide as she focused on something behind his back, and Coop's stomach dropped to his butthole, as it always did at the thought of pissing off that nutbag squirrel.

"He's behind me, isn't he?"

Her gaze met his, and she giggled. "No. I was having fun at your expense."

Leaning in to whisper into the shell of her ear, Coop said, "I plan to pay you back when you least expect it."

With a laugh and a wicked sparkle in her eye, she sashayed back to where Damian stood. "Let's get this show on the road, fellas. There's a secluded island awaiting my arrival."

The Aether lifted the Thorne family's metal wedding bowl, twirled a finger, and released the fragrant herbs of lavender and thyme into the air around them. Next, he dipped first Summer's ring, then Coop's into the bowl and handed them off to each of them. "These represent enduring love, devotion to one another, and the strength of commitment to the mate you've chosen to spend your life with. Please, exchange your rings in honor of your pledge."

After they were done and the rings were securely in place, Damian continued with a brief speech about upcoming trials and how they should face them together as a family. The white candles behind him flared high as if to emphasize his words as he encouraged them to honor their bond throughout time, with no exception. Next, he picked up the handfasting cloth.

"Summer, if you will?"

She placed her left hand in Damian's.

"Cooper?"

He mimicked the action.

Damian took their wrists, placed their palms together, and wove the cloth around them, then tied it off. The sharp zap they felt when their hands connected caused them both to gasp and jump.

"That's the merging of the Carlyle and Thorne lines through your bond," Damian explained. Meeting Summer's wide-eyed stare, he said, "Summer Thorne, I bind thee to Cooper Carlyle in this, a holy union. You shall honor and love him throughout all your days and beyond. Do you pledge to do so?"

"I do." Her voice was firm and confident, and the last remaining fear Coop had that this was all going to go to hell in a handbasket disappeared.

Damian faced him. "Cooper Carlyle, I bind thee to Summer Thorne in this, a holy union. You shall honor and love her throughout all your days and beyond. Do you pledge to do so?"

"I do."

The Aether covered their joined hands with his. "I ask the Goddess to bless this merging of souls. I ask her to protect and watch over them when they need it the most. And I ask her to grant them many years of wedded bliss."

Radiant light illuminated the lawn, nearly blinding Coop, for the span of ten seconds.

As it faded, Damian closed his eyes and whispered, "Blessed be."

"Blessed be," they echoed.

Damian gripped his hand and gave a little shake. "Coop, I encourage you to kiss your bride."

Cheers went up around them as they sealed their commitment with a passion-packed kiss that left Coop's brain matter a bowl of mush.

Summer was the first to recover, and she hugged Damian with a joyful laugh. "Thank you!"

"Entirely my pleasure, my dear."

Coop gathered what was left of his wits and addressed the Aether. "We're obliged."

"All any of us can ask is that you devote yourself to making her happy and raising your children in a loving environment." They shook hands. "Now, please, face the crowd."

They did as he directed.

"Ladies and Gentlemen, I present to you Mr. and Mrs. Cooper Carlyle."

THE RECEPTION WAS in full swing, and laughter floated around them as Coop held Summer close and danced to a soft, sultry tune. Her world felt complete. Not because she'd been longing to be married to Coop, although she had, but because in him, she'd found a partner to build a wonderful life with together. A man who was protective but understood she was self-suffi-cient and able to make her own decisions regarding her business and their child.

"What are you thinking about so hard?" he asked softly.

"You. Me. Us. How lucky I am."

"I'm the lucky one, sweetheart. I was blessed the day I met you, and giving you my ice cream cone was the smartest move I ever made."

"You were six. You didn't know you were even making a move," she returned with a laugh.

"True, but I knew, even then, that I'd do anything to dry your tears."

"Hmm, with the exception of your prom prank." Her tone was salty, but she ruined her act with a grin.

Coop touched his nose to hers. "You don't know it, but I was heartsick for months afterward. Seeing you sob, so silently and pitifully, as if your soul was shat-tered... God, Summer, it tore my guts up. I never want to see you unhappy again."

"It hurt to believe you didn't want me, Coop. But we were kids, and boneheaded moves were the norm in high school." She stretched up to drop a light kiss on his mouth. "And we're so far past that. We were a little slower than the average bears, but we worked through our misunderstandings. We created a beau-tiful baby girl who is the light of our lives, and we'll have another soul to spoil soon enough." Meeting his adoring gaze, she smiled and wiggled her ring finger. "And now, we're bonded, with enchanted rings to protect us. We've got this, babe."

"We've got this," he agreed. And with a deep chuckle, he spun her away from him and drew her back, tucking her against him once again. "I love you, Summer Carlyle."

"Summer Carlyle. I like the sound of that."

"Me, too."

"Do you think your grandmother is looking down on us and smiling, Coop?" Summer liked to think so. That somehow, long ago, the elderly woman had guessed how perfect the two of them would be together and did her best to encourage their union.

The air grew heavy with the smell of lemons, and Coop glanced around in surprise before meeting her startled gaze. "I think we have our answer, sweetheart."

Summer smiled in the face of his assured response and hugged him tighter as they swayed.

His lips brushed her ear, sending a shiver through her and sparking desire. "You didn't say it, Summer."

"Say what?"

"That you love me, too."

A little devil danced on her shoulder. "Are you sure? I could've sworn—"

He released a playful growl and tightened his arms.

"Okay, okay. I love you, too, Cooper Carlyle. Husband. Rocker of my world."

"Hmm. I like that—rocker of your world. Should we teleport the hell out of here so I can get to rocking?"

Heat coursed through her, and she almost agreed, but she didn't want to disappoint her guests. With a regretful sigh, she shook her head. "We still have to cut the cake and do the whole bouquet toss."

"Dammit, I hate tradition."

Laughing, Summer lightly slapped his chest. "You do *not*, Sheriff Traditional."

With a snort, he spun her around and dipped her. "For all you know."

"I happen to adore you that way. You're solid and dependable."

"You make me sound like an old shoe." Drawing her up, he gave her a mock glare.

She smirked. "Well, if the shoe fits…"

"Maybe I want to be more of a flip-flop. Did you ever think about that?"

"There's no flop in your flip, babe. And that's a good thing," she said with a bawdy wink.

His bark of laughter triggered hers. "Let's go cut that fucking cake so we can get out of here. My flip is straining the zipper of my pants."

With a snigger of appreciation for his responding humor, she pulled him toward the DJ. "Tell him to announce it." And seeing the wicked gleam in his eye, she slapped a hand over his mouth. "The cake cutting, not your strained-zipper issue."

"Your wish is my command, my darling wife."

"Yeah, and you'd better remember that."

"No doubt you'll remind me if I ever forget."

Summer laughed. "No doubt."

EPILOGUE

TEN YEARS LATER

a bloodcurdling scream rent the air.

From her lounge chair, Summer jerked into a sitting position and searched for the culprit. Pressing her hand to her heart, she reclined back. "Damned kids love giving me heart failure."

"Your drama-queen daughter especially," Tums replied with a hearty laugh. "I wonder what movie they're acting out now."

"Probably Braveheart or Tombstone. They're both Jolly's favorites, bloodthirsty beast that he is."

Autumn grinned affectionately at her son playing in the distance. "He does love a good battle."

"Pfft. I'm just happy we've been relatively battle free for the last ten years. I worry it could all change in a heartbeat."

"Don't borrow trouble, sister." But Autumn

entwined her fingers with Summer's and squeezed. They both remembered a time when their family fought for whatever bit of happiness they could get.

"Should we set the table? The others will be here soon," Summer said with a check of her watch.

"I suppose we should."

Just then, something caught Autumn's attention, and her expression darkened. Summer followed her gaze and saw the younger children were in a makeshift cage.

"Damn—"

"Don't swear!" Her sister ordered. "I've got this." Stalking off, Autumn bellowed her oldest son's name. Four faces turned in her direction, two decidedly guilty.

Biting her lip against laughter, Summer scowled and placed her hands on her hips in a show of solidarity for her sister when their children looked her way. With a wave of her hand, Olivia dissolved the bamboo cage containing Jolly's and her younger brothers.

"We're sorry, Aunt Tums. We were playing cops and robbers. Papa told us how he used to put the bad guys in prison."

Too far away to hear her sister's response, Summer turned her back and gave into silent laughter. Coop was going to get an earful when he returned from the animal clinic today.

The air around her contracted and grew heavy with magic, causing their group to stand stock still as they waited for the incoming witches to arrive.

The first to appear were Spring and Knox, who held a toddler on his hip and the hand of a five-year-old. The second their daughter saw her cousins, she was off and running.

"Slow down, Megan!" Knox called, wincing as his daughter face-planted in the grass. He handed off their son to Spring and ran to assist his disconcerted child. "Well, that didn't go as expected, did it?"

Megan, good-natured girl that she was, was quick to recover and gave her dad a solemn look. "It's okay, Daddy. I'm not hurt."

"I'll see for myself, thank you very much." He stood her up and, after dusting off the dirt, declared her perfect.

The adoration in Megan's eyes brought tears to Summer's and a lump to her throat. Knox and Spring deserved every happiness after the trials they'd faced to get to where they were, and the Goddess had blessed them.

"She'd rather die than cry in front of Knox," Spring said in a low voice. "She worries about disappointing him."

"At five?" Summer couldn't keep the surprise from her voice.

"In case you haven't noticed, she's accident prone,

and as athletic as Knox is, she fears he won't love her if she can't participate like the other kids in our family."

"You've both set her straight, I'm assuming?"

"We have. Still, she adores her dad." Spring smiled even as she shook her head in exasperation. "One day, she'll understand his love is unconditional. Hopefully, sooner rather than later."

"Give me my nephew. I need baby hugs." Taking Phillip from her sister, Summer rained kisses all over his sweet cherub face as he laughed and made smacking noises for more kisses.

"Your two are in the rebellious we-don't-want-mom-kisses-or-hugs stage?"

"Something like that."

Autumn joined them, trading places with Knox, who had apparently agreed to referee the herd.

"Give me my nephew—"

"Nope." Summer hugged Phillip tighter. "He's my date for the day."

"I thought I was." Coop's voice in her ear sent shivers down her spine.

Smiling her pleasure, she leaned back into him. "I miss when ours were this small."

"I'm not opposed to having more," he replied.

"I am. Two is plenty."

"Spoilsport." After a kiss to her temple and a surreptitious pat to her bottom, Coop sauntered away to hand a beer to Knox and accept a hug from Olivia.

"She still showers her father with affection," Summer said in a sour voice, though she wasn't truly upset.

"Face it, sister. Ollie is a daddy's girl." Autumn lifted Phillip from her arms and blew noisily against his neck as he giggled uncontrollably. "Not like our little man here. He's a total mama's boy. Isn't that right, my savory Philly Cheese Steak?"

"Yep!" Phillip chirped.

"He'd cop to murder if *you* asked him," Spring said with a laugh. "He adores his Aunt Tums."

"They all do." Summer shook her head. "I think she puts a spell on them to be their favorite."

"Oh, absolutely!" Winnie said, arriving in time to hear their conversation.

"They like me because I'm the fun aunt," Autumn retorted, flaring her eyes wide to make Phillip giggle.

"Pfft." Holding out her arms, Winnie smiled at their nephew. "But who makes the best cinnamon rolls?"

"Win-Win!" Phillip shouted as he dove into her arms.

Laughing, Summer shook her head. "You do realize he's going to charm everyone? You'll be beating his potential lovers off with a stick, Spring."

"Don't I know it. He's got his father's looks, and he's already started with that playful smirk. I'm doomed. Men and women alike are going to be lining the drive for one favorable smile from him."

They all laughed as Phillip demonstrated his smirk.

"Where are your gremlins, Winnie?"

"Zane is bringing the boys when they're done fishing. Keaton's with them, if I'm not mistaken."

"And Ava?"

"She wanted to help Mama in the kitchen. But truthfully, I think Uncle Alastair is sneaking her candy again." Winnie's warm smile proved she didn't mind. "If he is, I'm sending her home with them for the night, so I don't have to deal with a sugared-up child."

"They'd love it," Summer assured her. Turning to Autumn, she asked, "Is Chloe coming by?"

"I think so. She spent the night with Sabrina yesterday, but I received a text from her earlier saying they'd probably pop in at some point."

"Sweet. Holly told me Frankie has an art class, but she was hoping to see Chloe when they came by later."

The air around them crackled, and they all shared a look, knowing exactly who was about to arrive.

Between two towering oak trees, a thin gold band of light appeared. It grew in size and split to reveal the two teenagers, followed by Damian Dethridge. He paused in the opening and turned to look behind him, holding out his hand to someone they couldn't see. A minute later, his wife and son stepped through the rift with him, and it sealed shut behind them.

Nate Dethridge appeared uncertain and out of place as he watched the other children. From his pocket, he pulled an antique timepiece and flipped the lid open. With a nod far too serious for one so young, he snapped it shut and shoved it back into his pant pocket.

Summer hugged Vivian, then Damian. "Is he waiting for Delaney again?"

"Yes, Mack and Baz had a function, but intend to stop by in an hour or so. Poor Nate is beside himself when he's separated from her for any length of time." Damian shook his head as he wrapped an arm around his wife's waist. "But I can sympathize. Being apart from the woman you love is hell."

A small smile teased Vivian's mouth, but she didn't reply.

"I'll see if I can tempt him to play with the other children." Summer gestured toward the house. "Dad is in the kitchen with Mama."

"Are Preston and Selene here?" Vivian asked politely, reminding Summer of her deep friendship with Preston's wife.

"Nope. Not today. They are in Greece for their anniversary." Happy for them, Summer grinned. "But it's not like we don't have these little get-togethers every month. They'll be here for the next one, I'm sure."

"We'll go see if we can help your mother with anything." Damian nodded toward Chloe and Sabrina. "Please, keep them out of trouble. Teenage girls are too much for this old ticker of mine."

They all shared a laugh.

The day progressed as any family function would. There were minor skirmishes between children, scoldings from the parents of said children, and plenty of food and laughter to go around.

As Summer and Coop returned to the kitchen for coffee and a tray of Winnie's scrumptious cinnamon rolls, they shared a sweet, lingering kiss.

"I hope it's always like this," she said wistfully.

"It will be," he assured her in a deep, confident voice.

"I worry that as the kids grow and go off to college, days like these will become less frequent."

"Look at them, sweetheart." He turned Summer to gaze out over the backyard through the wide expanse of window. "We've all given them a solid foundation of love and support. They'll always return because, like us, they need one another. We're all one big family unit."

"But life—"

"Happens, yes." Coop hugged her from behind and rested his chin on the crown of her head. "Don't worry so much, okay? Alastair will always find a way to bring everyone together if they decide to stray."

And she knew his words to be true. As the patriarch of the Thorne family, Alastair would always keep his finger on the pulse of their lives, stepping in and redirecting them as necessary.

"I'm glad you finally figured that out, son." Alastair

stepped up to the counter and lifted the tray of coffee. "There's hope for you yet."

With that, he breezed out the door as quickly as he'd arrived.

Coop laughed.

At that moment, Summer had a vision of their future, and she joined her husband in his amusement. Yes, the next generation would face their own trials and tribulations, but they would all be just fine.

"Better bring out the cinnamon rolls before the natives get restless, my love." Summer stretched to kiss him one last time before handing him the tray of pastries. "I've something to check on."

He frowned his confusion. "What?"

"Never you mind."

With a final peck on her lips, he left the kitchen.

Heading for the stairs, Summer met Autumn at the base of the steps. "Hallmark?"

"Abso-freaking-lutely. I want to see what's happening between Chloe and Derek."

"But isn't she here?"

"Nope. After the Dethridges left, she teleported out," Autumn replied.

"Well, let's go scry. We have a romance to help along."

"You're becoming just like your father."

THANK you for reading Summer and Coop's happily ever after. If you want more of the Thorne family HEAs, be sure to look for the next book, **Boundless Magic**, featuring Autumn and Keaton, coming early 2024.

Turn the page for more of my stories.

ALSO BY T.M. CROMER

ABOUT THE AUTHOR

T.M. Cromer is a multi-award-winning, international best-selling author, who loves to craft wildly entertaining stories designed to keep you glued to your seat, turning the pages to find out what the hell happens next. She specializes in kickass heroines and the men who adore them.

Genres she writes include paranormal romance and romantic suspense.

Want to stay up to date on what's happening in the world of T.M. Cromer? Subscribe to her newsletter or text JOIN to 1-877-795-1526 to receive release news and promo alerts.

You can also join her VIP reader group on Facebook to chat with her, participate in polls, or just keep current on what's happening. Become a member today!

FOLLOW T.M. CROMER:

facebook.com/tmcromer

instagram.com/tmcromer

tiktok.com/@tmcromer

bookbub.com/authors/t-m-cromer

pinterest.com/tmcromer

amazon.com/stores/T.M.-Cromer/author/B011QK3WXY

Printed in the USA
CPSIA information can be obtained
at www.ICGtesting.com
LVHW021938061023
760372LV00015B/394

9 781956 941210